About This Novel

(Continued from online description)

Rob and Hannah Wilson (twins, 30) return home to Oregon from Europe in 2020 for their father's funeral. Dan Wilson, 70, rests in a green cemetery of twittering birds and sun-dappled shade, beside his second wife (or was she?) Nancy, who died in 2018 after thirty happy years together.

Unnoticed among two dozen mourners stands a beautiful, stylish angel named Claire from a parallel reality, wearing designer sunglasses and a Parisian outfit. Claire is the ghost of the twins' baby sister Klara, who died as an infant in 1979 while Dan Wilson served as a young U. S. Army soldier in Heidelberg, West Germany.

Klara's (Claire's) name is inspired by Paul Verlaine's exquisite 1869 poem *Clair de Lune*, or *Moonlight*, which inspired generations of artists, among them Claude Debussy who around 1890 composed a hauntingly beautiful classic piano piece. Readers are encouraged to get in the mood for this novel with (recommended) Claude Debussy's wonderful Third Movement (*Claire de Lune*) of his *Suite Bergamasque* at (e.g.) YouTube.

Ghostly Claire, at her father's funeral, looks classy and cool behind designer sunglasses. None of the mourners can see her, but she has a faint glow behind her, and is untouched by raindrops. Moving unseen through this story, otherworldly Claire plants Dan's journals and drops other clues to send Rob and Hannah on a mission: tying together loose ends and dead people in three parallel worlds. Claire's other gift will be to reveal the great secret of Leonardo's Mona Lisa, the world's most treasured and controversial art work (which could have gotten Leonardo burned at the stake by the Inquisition, had anyone realized; as Giordano Bruno was burned alive in the Campo di Fiori (Porticus of Octavia) in downtown Rome for alleged heresy in 1600, nearly a century after Leonardo's time.

Of Dan and Nancy Wilson's twin children, daughter Hannah works for a Paris insurance firm, and is dating young music producer Yves Cartier. Rob is a doctoral student at Frankfurt's Goethe University, dating Elise Gillen of Luxembourg.

Back in 1978, young Dan Wilson made a tragic decision on a famous bridge: the Pont des Arts near the Louvre Museum in Paris, where the Mona Lisa is housed. Before his death in 1518, Leonardo had lived his final years as guest in a French royal palace at Chambord, south of Paris. There, he worked endlessly at perfecting a second copy of the painting he originally delivered to a sponsor years ago in Italy, the husband of Lisa Gherardini in Florence. In our novel, we learn the final (scary) secret of Leonardo's devotion, that would have been fatal had the authorities figured it out. But, as with the deadly secrets of Nostradamus, the Inquisition's brutal and obsessive tyrants were not quite clever enough to see through the veils of deception. (I will soon publish a nonfictional, scholarly analysis of my theory about Nostradamus, but that is for another day).

Dan said goodbye to the love of his life, lovely Paris grad student Claudette Vervain. He returned to his duty station in Heidelberg, where he married a pretty but troubled Croatian-German girl named Stana Chetko, based on Stana's lies that she was pregnant by Dan.

Dan and Stana did conceive their daughter Klara (Claire) soon after.In a dark, forbidding mountain village near Heidelberg, Dan Wilson's emotional nightmare included a loveless marriage; infant Klara's death from a heart defect caused by Stana's drinking, depression, and not wanting a child; sociopathic bullying by Stana's father (an escaped Croatian Nazi war criminal who raped Stana as a child); and Dan's unsympathetic, ignorant, at times cruel U.S. Army superiors.

After his Army years, Dan returned to Oregon. He started a wonderful new life, marrying Nancy, and having the twins Rob and Hannah. But dark shadows of our past lie long upon the afternoon of a person's life.

In Paris, Claudette's doctoral thesis held stunning revelations on Leonardo da Vinci's art works in the Louvre, from notebooks of Dr. Benjamin Wandrous, a Jewish scholar murdered by the Nazis in occupied 1940s France. Soon after Dan left her, heart-broken Claudette dated a young alcoholic, with whom Claudette died in a car crash, and her wonderful discoveries were lost.

Fate, however, works with angels sometimes to fix unbearable situations. On the windy, weepy, rainy 1979 night as Klara died at the German medical center in Heidelberg, a marvel happened in the village miles away as her broken-hearted father slept exhaustedly. He awoke in darkness, sat on the bed, and heard a calm, strong woman's voice in his head. He instantly knew it was his baby daughter, but as a mature woman (somehow, somewhere in time…).

Klara (Claire) assured him, in the totally composed, self-assured voice of a successful and strong adult woman, that everything would be fine. Despite that mysterious reassurance, based on a true story, Dan Wilson would grieve for his daughter's death the rest of his life. In that auditory visitation (no vision), she promised that one day in the future, at the moment of his death, her daddy wouild receive a wonderful gift. He would have a chance at a second life, to undo his dark error in leaving Claudette; he would return as a young man to that bridge, the Pont des Arts near the Louvre. Instead of leaving; starting his life over from that moment, he would hold Claudette tightly, and never let her go. And of course, in that world, Hannah and Rob would never be born, but Dan and Claudette would raise a different family of children who would grow up in Paris.

In the course of these wondrous events, we learn the final secret of eternallyh famous artist Leonardo Da Vinci. The world would learn the true secret of Leonardo's obsession with the portrait of Lisa Gherardini, a rather ordinary housewife in 1500s Florence. Lisa Gherardini del Giocondo's portrait hangs in the Louvre, insured at a record billion Euros. Touched by her own tragedy and joys clearly visible, forever codified in her eyes and enigmatic smile, Mona Lisa gazes at us from a lost world with a melancholy but courageous visage, a woman who lived a full, hard life centuries ago. Leonardo's obsession as a Renaissance artist and scientist went far beyond her humanity to a spiritual plane. Had anyone known, he'd have been burned as a heretic or witch in a dark and cruel world.

In the famous Shakespeare & Company bookstore on the Left Bank, on her journey, Hannah bumps into her lost sister's ghost for the first time under a sign that reads: "Be not unkind to strangers, lest they turn out to be angels."

Louvre Museum, Paris

Pont des Arts – Passerelle

Leonardo Da Vinci's
Dangerous Dream:
Mona Lisa   Moon Goddess
a Fantasy Novel of Historical Inquiry
by Jean-Thomas Cullen

Seine

CONTENTS

Clair de Lune
(Moonlight)

Your tender soul is a twilight landscape
where masques and bergamasques dance,
plucking strings; looking oh so slightly
    sad in happy costumes,

    as they sing in some minor clef
about finding love and happiness.

Their song weaves melancholy
    with moonlight...

    ...quiet moonlight so sad and so lovely
that it makes birds dream in their trees,
while fountains sob in ecstasy
    'mid slender pillars and marble statues.

-- Paul Verlaine
Paris, 1869
Translated by Jean-Thomas Cullen 2017

Translation (previous page) was completed 2017 by Jean-Thomas Cullen.

This classic 1869 poem by Paul Verlaine (1844-1896) was, and remains, a monument to his times, to the Decadent and Symbolist and *fin de siècle* movements, and many others who would lay claim to its quietly melancholy magic and power.

Verlaine's contemporaries—composers like Claude Debussy and Gabriel Fauré—put it to music. A great deal of creative activity centered around Paris at the turn of the century, even while many great artists flourishing in Paris came from around France (e.g., Arthur Rimbaud, Maurice Ravel) and greater Europe (Alphonse Mucha, Rainer Maria Rilke), not to mention U.S. personalities like Henry James and T.S. Eliot. Later, Ernest Hemingway, F. Scott Fitzgerald, and other U.S. figures joined the magic at such Parisian locales as Shakespeare & Company. Much of this is relevant to the expression and mood of this story by Jean-Thomas Cullen.

Verlaine's title seems to point toward an old French folk song (*Au Clair de Lune*) but, as this novel suggests, our fascination with moonlight is primordial and in our DNA. This is evident as well in the notebooks and works of Leonardo da Vinci, whose immortal painting *Mona Lisa* or *La Gioconda* has a place of honor in the Louvre Museum in Paris.

Paul Verlaine was not the only great artist of the late 19th Century to write, paint, or compose on the theme of moonlight. His famous poem inspired many other artists.

This author's favorite example is Claude Debussy's 1890ish *Suite Bergamasque*, whose third of four movements is titled *Clair de Lune*. That quietly haunting music is particularly suited to the mood of this novel as the story ascends from darkness into light.

Other classic works of similar theme abound, both before and after Verlaine's time.

As early as 1802, Ludwig van Beethoven completed his Piano Sonata No. 14 (Moonlight Sonata, styled a Fantasia) in a similarly pensive, quietly whimsical mode.

Other famous composers of delicate nocturnes of similar title included Gabriel Fauré in 1887 (Opus 46, Two Songs) which appears as Movement Six in his 1919 (*Opus 112: Masques et Bergamasques*).

Victor Hugo wrote a poem by that title, Guy de Maupassant published a short story anthology by that title in 1884, and a long list of other artists and composers approached the same theme from their various directions.

The terms *masque* and *bergamasque* refer to traditional styles of harlequin or busker costumes and dances, especially in French and Italian (Bergamo) cultures.

Part One

Journal III
Time of Separation

Oregon 1980-2020

1.   Prolog: Cemetery

The one generation passes, and the next generation becomes master of the next...

So intoned the priest at Dan Wilson's funeral, as the coffin was about to be lowered so that the deceased could rest beside his wife who had predeceased him in 2018. Now was summer 2020. Dan and Nancy had shared over thirty glowing years, during which they were graced with two fine children who made those passing decades time well spent.

The twins—brother and sister—Rob and Hannah Wilson had flown in from Europe for their father's funeral—Hannah from Paris, Rob from Frankfurt. They stood together with two dozen other mourners in a gray, chilly cemetery, under massively weeping willow trees, near the foggy coast at Newport, not far south and west of Salem, Oregon.

Standing among the darkly dressed men and women mourners was an angel named Claire. The angel (a messenger, a ghost) looked like any other living, grieving friend or family member, and went almost unnoticed. Hannah would remember her later, when the veil of memory was lifted over her father's life and affairs.

Rob and Hannah were each still single. They were handsome, dark-haired, well-off young career persons of thirty, wearing finely but conservatively tailored clothing with belted and buckled tan raincoats over charcoal suits. Since they were fraternal twins, the close match of their clothing would not surprise anyone who knew them. Their parents had raised them lovingly and intelligently, although there had always been a vague sense of something missing in that happy marriage of Daniel Wilson and Nancy Everol-Wilson. But then, Hannah figured, every life has those lost puzzle pieces, those morning-after what-ifs, maybes and wannabes.

Her brother Rob held a woman's (their late mother's, in fact) mauve umbrella over both of them, while Hannah huddled close, with her arm slung through his. Each stifled many a sob as they now buried their father in a grave beside their mother, who had predeceased him by two years.

The large granite rectangle before them bore twin plaques in greenish-gray slate, one of which read *Daniel Robert Wilson 1950-2020* and the other *Nancy Everol-Wilson 1950-2018.* A dark iron banner on the broad slab, almost like a twin bed for Dan and Nancy, proclaimed: *They rest in eternal peace.* A precious little angel, molded in marble-dust Art Deco style, presided over the headstone, and seemed to weep as rainwater runneled down its blackened nose and cheeks.

Angel Claire had special reason to be there among the mourners, since Dan Wilson had been her father as well. Claire (or, in German, Klara) had become a ghost long before Rob or Hannah were born, so they had never met her—yet. She would be thirteen years older than the twins. She was, like Rob and Hannah, of slightly above medium height, slender, and elegant. Her hair was dark-golden blonde, straight and cut just above the shoulders, rather than dark-haired and bobbed like Hannah's.

Claire brought with her a barely visible, otherworldly glow; it was not a halo surrounding her, but she appeared somehow faintly backlit. Claire had blue-green eyes like Rob and Hannah. The mourners could see her, but did not notice her or remember her. She wore a pearly gray raincoat over a plum-colored dress with low-heeled beige pumps. The well-dressed ghost seemed to signal that she was tall enough, and did not want to advertise her presence with stylish high heels. But of course one of her talents was to be in a crowd and not be noticed, despite being quietly, devastatingly attractive. She did not need an umbrella. Her hair and skin remained untouched by the drizzle that made everyone else soggy that morning.

Hannah was busy with her thoughts and memories. Another racking sob escaped her as she remembered how her father had been declining, and seemed to retreat into a fantasy world when she'd last been home with him. He would stare into space and mumble about some decision he'd made on a bridge, and it was time to make it all different. As if he or anyone else could go back, and change the past, or forge a new timeline somehow. And of course Hannah so regretted now that she had not spent more time with him these last months. What had Daddy said in his last sad, mumbling two years of life? "There are chapters yet to be written in this story, trust me."

The heavy, rain-slick, glistening coffin went into the ground, lowered by wet-looking, bedraggled cemetery workers in rubber slickers, who were glad to get it over with and return to their dry office and workshop just inside the front entrance.

Heavy fog hung over the Pacific coast just west of them that morning. The air smelled fresh, of damp lilacs and sweet greenery. Somewhere, a dove cooed on a leafy-sheltered tree branch. Dan and Nancy Wilson had been laid to rest, and the ground would close over them in eternal peace. It remained now for the twins, each in their own city and life in Europe, to process these matters and seek closure; and they knew it would take time.

80 • 03

An aunt, an uncle, a cousin, and a co-worker of their late father, along with the parish priest, walked with Hannah and Rob on the gravel path leading from the cemetery into a narrow street among tall hedges and weeping willow trees.

Family and friends gathered at a restaurant for a warming meal to take the chill out: onion soup, salad, beef stew with carrots and potatoes thicked with broccoli, buttered toast to dip, and several desert choices. The atmosphere, despite torn and grieving emotions, was familial and cozy. The twins had finished college in Portland, Rob in international business and Hannah in international relations, and their work lives had taken them to Europe a half dozen years ago—Rob in Germany, Hannah in France. They were fluent in their languages, and were working on dual citizenship. *Comfortable* would describe how they felt.

Hannah had flown in from Paris, where she worked at a large insurance firm in the western end of the city in the cleanly modernistic, industrial *la Defense* sector with its skyscrapers, parks (of course), and gigantic arch for the new century. Her brother, Daniel Robert, was usually called Rob to avoid confusion with their father's name, Dan. Mom (Nancy) had named him Rob. Mom had passed away two years ago from leukemia at age 68.

Rob had arrived from Frankfurt two days before the funeral. He'd picked Hannah up at the airport in his stylish dark-blue Mercedes yesterday. They'd spent their last day, each in their old bedrooms like old times—and sharing a bathroom in to yell at each other about the toothpaste and other petty issues—in the house where they had grown up. Hannah would fly out later today, while Rob would stay one or two extra days to sort out some remaining possessions and settle paperwork with the real estate agents who would put the house on the market now. They expected a quick sale, since it was a storybook little middle-earth home. The twins had family in Oregon, and planned to visit at least once a year, but for now their passions and interests lay in Europe (including a nice looking guy for Hannah in Paris, named Yves; and an attractive Luxembourg girl named Elise for Rob, working with Rob in Frankfurt, a slightly over a four-hour haul by train or car from Paris. As Rob had calculated, consider that it's about two hours from Portland Oregon to Eugene Oregon; and four hours gets you from Seattle close to Eugene—so Europe is a small world compared to North America.

ಐ • ೞ

Funeral finished and forever behind them (so they thought), Rob and Hannah sat elbow to elbow and reminisced over checkered tablecloths and smeared, empty pasta dishes and vinegary-oily salad plates well-cleaned. Other family members sat around them—beloved cousins, aunts, uncles, a long-ago grammar school teacher, the priest, and other mainstays of a stable youth in a small sort of middle-earth community.

"I wish I could have been here the last week," said Hannah. She had flown in a few months ago during Dad's final illness, but couldn't afford any long absence from her job as an office manager in *La Défense* business district just west of the city. She'd had to return to work, only to fly back again for the funeral.

Rob's story was the same, except his work destination had been Frankfurt, Germany. "You've got your life to life," Rob said comfortingly. "Dad would want you to carry on. We'll always think of them."

"I know," she said with a sigh. "I miss mom too."

"She's been gone two years now." Rob said it in an ironic tone, as if he couldn't quite believe it. "Two years already."

"Dad was talking strange stuff the last little while," Hannah ventured.

"Yeah. He said something like the story isn't over. Whatever he meant."

"You think he was losing it?"

Rob shook his head. "Hard to say. Dad was a tough guy."

She pressed: "But how did he seem the last few weeks? You were here."

Rob thought for a moment, bit his lip. "I think he was lucid. But your're right; he was saying some strange things."

"Like what?"

"I'm not sure. That there was a promise, and he was ready to cash in on it at last. He'd waited a long time, paid his dues, stuff like that. I have no idea what he was talking about."

She nodded, hurting inwardly. "He said something about mom when I last was here. Like he waited it out, whatever that means."

"They loved each other," Rob quickly said. Dad could not have meant it as it sounded—that he had endured his marriage and his children. He'd been too devoted and loving a man for that to be true. *Waiting it out* almost sounded as if he'd been waiting for some next chapter to unfold in the afterlife—totally absurd.

"They did love each other," Hannah said, almost a tiny bit unsure. Their parents had been married nearly thirty years. They bickered their fair share, and often just seemed detached and like two lone cats prowling around in a common home. Rob and Hannah had done plenty of sibling bickering as well. *The family that bickers together stays together.*

Especially since Rob and Hannah had grown up, gone to college, and had gone their own separate ways. Mom was always doing things by herself or with her lady friends, and he kept busy with his activities. Almost like she and Dad just lived in the same house together, maybe were friends, but there wasn't as much passion as Hannah might have expected. But then their parents had been married a long time, so you had to be there to understand how that worked. All you had to do was think of schoolmates whose parents had gone through (always) damaging divorces, or a parent died, that sort of thing, to realize how lucky you were. Same little house, same bushes and lantern in the driveway, same house number, for their entire lives.

Rob summed it up: "It was a loving marriage. Just sort of toned down and quiet."

She nodded. "I was happy growing up."

They paused a second, not meeting each other's eye. There had always been a certain dark and uncertain *thing*, no bigger than a molecule, buzzing around the best of times. They knew Dad had come back from his Army tours in Germany a broken man, and had gone through a long readjustment hell before meeting Nancy.

"So was I." He put his hand over his sister's. "We were very fortunate. They loved us and did everything for us, and we loved them. What more can anyone ask?"

"We were very lucky," she agreed. Even as she visited with friends and family, including her twin brother, she began packing and planning to return to Paris. Speaking of chapters: here was another chapter closed.

C'est la vie. That's life. Nothing is perfect but…

Life goes on.

2.   Hannah Returns To Paris

Hannah was no fan of air travel, having done too much of it already at the seasoned age of thirty.

The trip was, as always, a long flight back on Air France to Paris from Portland PDX with a change of planes at Heathrow, London. She found no particular pleasure in the grueling twelve hour flight, cramped into the common area by a window overlooking sun-gilded, orangey cumulus clouds much of the way. Her one consolation was the idea of getting back to the home she had made, the job that sustained her at a major insurance company, and her boyfriend Yves Cartier who was a video producer for television ads and up and coming music acts. She closed her eyes, sat back, and dreamed of Yves like a pill to ease the discomfort of travel.

ဢ • ဣ

Yves was her age, thirty, tall, handsome, and slender with a body that snapped like a whip. He had grown up in a medium-sized, ancient town north of Paris called Beauvais, in the Oise region of northern France. He'd qualified to attend university in Paris, studying business administration, and now ran his modest but promising business. She'd known Yves for a year, and was comfortable with his character and personality. He was pretty much a low-key, straight-arrow guy. Like Hannah, he came from a small town and steadfast family, simply on a different continent; and was determined to mold his own life with the same quietly hard-pressing ambition. It was way to early to know which way the proverbial wind was blowing for 'them' (Hannah smiled to herself: is there a 'we'? Is the answer 'oui'?); but they were comfortable together.

After losing both of her parents in the past two years, besides having voluntarily displaced herself so far from home, Hannah appreciated the steady touch. Her brother Rob was just a few hours away by car or fast train. And Yves was always good for comfort at the right moment, and at other moments excitement when they needed it, whether to go dancing at night spots in the Marais, or a weekend trip to Geneva or Brussels or wherever. That was a major beauty of living in Europe in the middle of so much history and culture, without losing sight of all that was wonderful back home.

Hannah half-slept or dozed much of the way on her British Airways flight to London, and then remained groggily awake for the final hour or so flying into Orly in the southeast of Paris, ironically on British Airways. Paris was overcast—gray and chilly—as she emerged with her suitcase and two handbags, and took a cab home to her small studio on the other side of Paris. She was paying a thousand euros a month for a tiny studio, but she wasn't complaining. It was furnished, on an upper floor in a solid old 19th Century bloc in Auteuil and Passy, 16th Arrondissement. Above all, it was clean, safe, and quiet. Not to mention private, not that she did crazy stuff like dance in her underwear or bake naked in the kitchen while gyrating to loud music. She was a quiet tenant, and appreciated coming home, closing the door, and feeling cozy in her nest.

When the cab dropped her off, it was all she could do to lug her stuff up three narrow flights of stairs, lock the door, and throw herself face-down spread-eagled on the bed, in her clothes, to fall asleep.

With good timing, she awoke at dawn, made herself a light breakfast of yoghurt, fruit, coffee, and toast with butter and jam, and felt ready for work. She was still a bit bone-weary, partly from the stress and loss, and partly from the long cramped trip. But she was glad to be home and moving on. She had the day off, but looked forward to returning to work.

She felt at ease on the Métro, about a half hour ride each way between home and work. That allowed her to sit idly and look out the window, or study the other passengers while the train windows threw alternate lozenges of light and shadow across everyone's features. Or she might keep her head down, and read on the Android *tablette* she carried in her purse.

Her workday in La Defense was satisfying enough. The odd name of the business district west of Paris dated to a time, in past centuries, when the French capital was surrounded by military defenses to resist invasion and occupation.

Her job paid well, with total benefits including universal health care, paid vacations, benefits, and other human rights unlike her contemporaries back in the USA. She found working in Paris at a multi-lingual job to be challenging, but fun. It kept her in the company of many interesting expats who all adored living in Paris, despite its good and bad points—French, European, North American, Asian, South American. There was a sort of United Nations of skilled, intelligent workers recruited by this European Union insurance giant that had linkages on all other continents and their huge corporations as well. She enjoyed the diversity at her company—you could almost be a citizen of this global corporation; *scary thought*. Part of her clung to her notions of small town living in the U.S., but that was now just a back door.

Her brother Rob was working in finance while finishing his interdisciplinary doctorate in Humanities at Goethe University in Frankfurt, and had many passionate comments to make about current events as well as history. Of late, Hannah was happy to hear that Rob had a beautiful and intelligent girlfriend, who was working for the same firm in Frankfurt as a financial analyst. Hannah looked forward to meeting Elise Gillen. Elise was from Luxembourg-ville (Luxembourg City), capital of the tiny nation, which, despite its size, was a full fledged and founding mmember of both the European Union and the United Nations. Hannah regularly got selfies and ussies from the two, so she could be satisfied that Rob was taking a very nice path in life.

ᘒ ● ᘓ

Though touched by occasional moments of grief or melancholy at the loss of both parents, and of the house in Salem, Hannah threw herself into the business of being at home in the 16th Arrondissement (of a total twenty such districts) on the Right Bank of the Seine. From her tiny apartment in Auteuil (if she owned a car, which she didn't, but you could taxi or Yves) it would be a ten minute drive on a good day with little traffic to reach the Eiffel Tower in the Champs de Mars in the 15th Arrondissement across the river. The Yves thing was a little fond joke between her and Yves. Before meeting him, she'd take a cab (Uber, whatever); now she'd take an Yves. And he of course, typically nuzzling behind her ear and ready to make love at any moment, was only too happy to provide all the Yves she needed, until he tickled and she squealed to get away, until he caught up with her and overwhelmed her with affection that she so deeply loved.

She was on her tablette with Yves the minute she got off the plane that evening. He was quickly there to pick her up from De Gaulle and drive her home on the Périphérique (circumferential highway around the city) while they chatted excitedly in a mix of French and English, happy to be reunited. As he drove, she kept a hand on his thigh as if to make sure he couldn't get away, and she admired him in the light of passing street lamps. Just as often, she'd catch him stealing admiring glances at his *belle Américaine*. They were a bit of a catch for each other, each in their own way. He was as close to the storybook French *beau* she could have imagined as a girl back in Salem. His male and female friends, and family, found her charmingly cosmopolitan without losing what made her uniquely a U.S. American, including her quaint ideas about women's rights and all that sort of *puritanisme* obsessively driving U.S. minds in their opinions. Like all good people everywhere, they were prepared to adapt, adjust, and learn, just as she was doing, so they all got along well.

Along that highway route, looking forward maybe to a hot bath together followed by lots of *oo-la-lah*, she smiled quietly. She looked forward to sitting on the Métro that first morning back to work. Even more, she though happily of the nice personalities multiplying in her life here in Europe (Rob, Elise, Yves, and the people close to them). She was developing a bit of a family around herself, and it was nice. Now that Rob was latched up with Elise, it would be fun to double-date. She thought: *two is twins, three is awkward, but four is a party. Let's dance.*

೮೦ • ೦೪

Dancing was exactly what she and Yves did the next evening when they were done with work. Since they both lived in the 16th, it was easy to get together. She had a tiny flat way up, while Yves had a little basement studio let to him by wealthy relatives who owned property in Passy (very expensive).

Yves was still struggling financially, and she was paycheck to paycheck. He'd just finished a 10,000 Euro contract for an up and coming rock group, so it meant a great deal to her when he treated her to dinner in a nice Marais restaurant on a narrow, winding street of small shops. They tarried over a light dinner of tiny pork medallions with small boiled potatoes, asparagus, and marinated red beets. Dessert came in the form of apricot brandies.

Hannah and Yves went dancing, had a bit more to drink than they should have, and took the Métro to his studio in Passy. They left his car at a curb near a cozy little bar in the Épinettes neighborhood. Better gamble on a parking ticket if that happened, he figured, rather than a very costly drunk driving arrest. They had a fun trip home and crashed in his flat in Passy.

Life was getting back to normal, except for a few stray moments of grief, and strangely some weird incidents. What had the psychologist Karl Jung written in the middle of the last century? That there are coincidences in life that are bound together by synchronicity, meaning you may not find a cause of B as a result of A, but A and B are related meaningfully in the nebula or cloud of self-understanding by which the individual navigates through life.

೮೦ • ೦೪

One day about a week after returning from the USA, on a Sunday afternoon, she was waiting for Yves to finish a recording gig and pick her up in his cool wheels at one of her favorite spots: the little green park Square de René Viviani within a softball's throw of the famous Shakespeare & Company bookstore in the 5th Arrondissement (relocated from its 1922 origin in the 6th). She had gotten a cup of takeout coffee from the bookstore's café, and sat enjoying a sunny moment with a light breeze. She had found a seat on a little park bench on the south side, with the church of St. Julian the Poor (St. Julien le Pauvre) at her back. The *square* (a borrowed English word, meaning tiny pocket-parks in Paris) had at its center a picturesque slightly sunken octagon area with steps and flowers and a fountain in the center. The square was surrounded by an iron fence and tall bushes, and served as a peaceful spot in the bustle of the major Quai de Montebello directly north, over which loomed the twin towers of Notre Dame de Paris.

It was one of her favorite places in the world, an oasis of peace. Being a bit of an egghead, Hannah often liked to sit in the Shakespeare & Company Bookstore on the Rue de la Bûcherie. She read on many topics, and one of her avid interests lay in the history of Paris itself. From the Square de Rene Viviani, where she sat in the little park, you walked out the wrought-iron gate onto the sidewalk, hung a left, and walked about thirty feet to a tiny cobblestone street (Rue Saint Julien le Pauvre, named for a nearby church). You crossed over a pedestrian zone no more than about six feet across, the width of a standard ancient Roman post road (this was the heart of ancient Roman Paris, the Latin Quarter). At that point, a little street dog-legged off the Quai de Montebello in this old Medieval church quarter. The little street, also cobblestone, was the Rue de la Bûcherie, supposedly named for workshops centuries ago, where logs (*des bûches*) were brought into the city on the Seine, to a *port des bûches* near here, then carried to the workshops on this little street, and cut up for building purposes in the ever-growing city. Having read that it was also a place, centuries ago, where spoiled meat was brought to be boiled and salted to feed the poor, she thought you had to wonder if the name did not almost as likely come from *bouche*, mouth; an idle thought, she groused; another fork in reality and alternate worlds. She shook her head to clear it and drive away an odd moment of déjà vu.

As she was sipping coffee, enjoying the breeze and sunshine in a little reverie while awaiting Yves to pull up at the curb outside the park, she heard a faint rustling sound beside her on the bench. Startled, because she thought she was alone, she turned and saw something she had not noticed until that moment. Beside her on the bench lay a brochure in English.

She glanced around. Had someone walked by? Had the wind blown it beside her, making that slight sound, because she could swear the brochure was not there when she sat down.

Idly, holding her coffee to one side, she picked up the brochure with her free hand, and glanced through its folded pages (it was a single large sheet). Oddly, for just a moment, she got a shiver up and down her spine. There was almost a moment in which the sunlight darkened and then lightened again, as if an angel had passed by, dropped this beside her for a reason, and moved on to disappear into the bright light and busy traffic on the frontage road Quai de Montebello.

Before stuffing the brochure into her purse to read later, she noticed it was from the Louvre, specifically about the wing in which hung Leonardo da

Vinci's *Mona Lisa*—the most famous and expensive painting in the world, as the brochure proudly related. The painting was valued for insurance purposes at nearly one billion euros. Someone had placed a stray red crayon mark (why?) on the last page, at a footnote dedicated to the long-ago research of one Professor Benjamin Wandrous. Before being deported and murdered at Auschwitz by the Nazis in 1944, this man was researching the secrets of Leonardo da Vinci, who spent his final years in France. The Renaissance genius from Florence had been brought north by his final patron, an appreciative King François I in 1516, to perform some projects (not the *Mona Lisa*, which Leonardo worked on passionately at no pay for the last decade or so of his life). Leonardo lived and worked at the Château d'Amboise in the Loire Valley until his death in 1519 at age 67 (most likely from stroke and other cardiovascular conditions). So he was a French painter in his last years, rather than Italian; and his famous *Mona Lisa* became property of the French king. What was the secret of Leonardo's passion for the mysteriously smoky (sfumato) painting and its subject, a sweet but rather average-looking, almost plump young housewife who lived in downtown Renaissance Florence with her wealthy husband? What was the secret of that slight, otherworldly smile that the world has admired and puzzled about for centuries? Lisa Gherardini's smile had become the most famous and mysterious in the world. And her image was insured for the highest price of any painting in history—upward of a billion euros.

Hannah shrugged, stuffed the brochure away, and forgot all about it.

For the moment.

3. Rob Finds Journal, Travels to Paris

Rob Wilson was on Skype daily with the new love of his life, Elise Gillen. She was from Luxembourg City, where her parents still lived in the Upper or Old City neighborhood of Limpertsberg, complete with remnants of cobbled sidewalks from long ago. The U.S. Embassy was in that tree-lined area, along with many fancy villas. Elise was a brunette with long, straight hair, chestnut, that glowed reddish in sunlight. She had beautiful dark eyes that could stare soulfully. *She speaks with her eyes half the time*, Rob thought.

He'd seen Hannah off to her plane at the Portland International Airport (PDX) and returned to Salem to wrap up some of Dad's remaining affairs. Dan Wilson, without saying much to anyone, had recognized his impending departure and put his affairs in order. He'd left his papers neatly boxed and arranged for easy reading. The kids (Rob and Hannah) had already inherited jewelry, a painting or two, and other valuables from Nancy directly. Rob was puzzled, somewhere deep in his heart, but could not put his finger on what was bothering him. His mother had been quiet and reserved in her own way, but he had the feeling she'd kept no secrets. It was all out front with Nancy. Dad, on the other hand, had lived a more complicated life. For one thing, Nancy had married late, in her thirties, and had enjoyed a long afternoon of love, so to speak. Dan, on the other hand, had traveled a lot in his youth, including a long stint in the U.S. Army in Europe. There had been a shadowy, frightening first marriage to a German woman whose name Rob didn't even recall. Dad had hardly ever talked about it, but it was clear it had been a dark two or three years in his life. There had been a baby, name again unknown, born with some congenital illness—heart defect, Rob seemed to recall Dad mentioning once or twice—who died at less than one year old in the great German medical center in Heidelberg. A lot of dark and awful drama had occurred near Heidelberg, the picturesque and historic city on the Neckar River, where Dad had been stationed as a junior enlisted man in the 1970s. He had returned a broken man, a lost soul, and taken a decade in Portland and Salem to put his life back together. Which he had, in the end, falling in love with steadfast, true-blue Nancy. And yet there always seemed to be a piece missing with him. Once, during a stormy argument between Hannah and Dad, Rob had sought comfort with his mother. Nancy had been steady-state as always, saying, "You know he often has bad dreams and wakes up in terror and cold sweat." And once Dad had confided that there was a dream he often had, in which he was back in West Germany of the 1970s, walking the streets of the moderately small town near Heidelberg in which the U.S. Army at that time occupied an old 1700s vintage Pfälzisch (Palatinate) army Kaserne (barracks) with cobblestone streets, yellow turrets, and a mix of blue slate and orange brick roofing tiles.

Aunt Molly (Dad's sister and only surviving sibling) and Uncle Stan, who lived in the East Lancaster section of town, came by with a van to pick up the boxes and other effects. One of the last moments for Rob, in the house where he had grown up along with Hannah, was to hand the keys to a pleasantly eager man and woman real estate agent team. The plan was to do a light renovation and then sell the house quickly during the current slight upturn in market values.

Rob gave the house a fond and wistful pat on the side as he walked down the driveway to a waiting private cab. He wished the house a happy future, and many more playing, screaming, growing children.

Time to go. Time to let go.

He picked up Dad's old brown leather briefcase, which he planned to carry back to Europe with him. It was full of papers and photos—including a mysterious Journal III. Bidding farewell to Molly and Stan, he let the stranger drive him to the airport. It was an odd feeling, riding with a nice but unknown man who appeared to be a recent immigrant. The man told him during light conversation that he was of German-Samoan origin, and had been a U.S. citizen all his life. So much for guessing where people came from these days. Rob told him he had grown up in Salem, and wished him well. Never learning the man's name, he shook hands heartily at the airport entrance, and wished him well. Inwardly, he felt similarly to when he'd said goodbye to the old house. Take good care of my city, he thought, as he strode across the concourse sidewalk with the briefcase in one hand, and gave a final wave with his free other hand.

℘ • ℭ

During the long flight, Rob dozed a bit. He ate the light lunch they served, and enjoyed a hot cup of black coffee over Greenland. As the line of day and night crawled slowly past—meaning it was like dusk for at least four hours while the Airbus and the nightfall line raced each other eastward—Rob opened the briefcase and began reading Dad's Journal III. He was puzzled. Why Journal III? Had there been Journals I and II? Or had Dad simply gotten a deal years ago at a stationery store on this particular fancy book. It was an old, worn black notebook with cheaply gilded edges. Nothing fancy. Two hundred pages inside, stitched with white thread, were standard-ruled with faint blue horizontal lines. Each page also had a faint red vertical line to make the left margin, like a zillion other notebooks Rob had seen. It was an old notebook, stuffed with loose papers and an occasional photo. There was Hannah on her first bicycle at age seven, missing her two upper front teeth and smiling sun-blinded on a summer day on the sidewalk outside the old house. There he was, Rob, kneeling on the grassy front lawn and playing with one of the series of mostly golden-orange retriever mutt mixes they'd had over the years. He flipped the photo over, but the dog's name wasn't on it, just his own written in Mom's precise hand: David Robert Wilson, 6 yrs old. That brought a little mist to his vision. He wiped with one finger, and gave forth a soggy sniffle. This was an emotional time. Hannah would probably need a hankie when they got around to sitting in her place in Paris or his place in Frankfurt with these records before them. Near as she could figure, Journal III was a record and scrapbook of Dan Wilson's final forty years spent in Salem, Oregon after returning from years stationed in Europe.

4.   Chronology of Dan's Life (Journal III)

Rob and Hannah next saw each other neither in Paris nor in Frankfurt but in Luxembourg two weeks later. Rob was back to work, feeling grounded, had everything running smoothly, and could afford a three day weeked to visit with his sister. Hannah told him that she, too, was glad to be back in the saddle, resuming her own life, and pursuing her romantic interest with Yves Cartier.

Rob called as Hannah and Yves were each having a glass of wineon her tiny balcony. They sat with their legs entwined, facing each other amid flowerboxes overflowing with red blossoms, and enjoying a long, lazy afternoon. The sun was hidden in a hazy, golden-cloudy sky as the western suburbs of Paris rustled with traffic in a light wind. On a clear day, she got a faint glimpse of the very top of the Eiffel Tower's spidery girders.

"Where are you?" Hannah asked with her Droid in one hand and a wine glass in the other, while Yves (looking humorously seductive) cradled her bare feet in his. The balcony was barely large enough for the two of them plus a tiny round table. They were half-shielded by the flowers and wrought-iron railings. As she spoke, Yves wriggled his toes against hers, and she wriggled back in a whimsical code.

"Frankfurt," Rob said far away. "We're driving down to Luxembourg, and I thought maybe you and Yves could meet us there. It's almost halfway."

"Yes, that's right," she said. "How halfway is it exactly?"

"Frankfurt to Luxembourg is a three hour drive, and Paris to Luxembourg is about four hours. So we can each do about half of a run for one of us to drive between Paris and Frankfurt."

"Let me ask Yves what he's doing this weekend." She lowered the phone and swatted his foot. "Be serious for a second. You want to go to Luxembourg?"

Yves frowned, wrinkling his lightly tanned face with its overhanging curly, short brown hair. "Eh? Why not."

She told him, "I don't feel like driving by myself. Otherwise, I could just hop a train and be there in the same time."

Yves shrugged. "For you, anything. It's a nice little city, and I haven't been there in years."

"Okay," she told Rob. "It's a deal."

ಬಿ • ಉ

On Saturday morning, Hannah and Yves packed a weekend satchel each, which they tossed into the trunk of his Mercedes sedan.

She wore a loose, white-and-faded-blue striped cotton summer dress with white strapped sandals; plus sunglasses and a yellow silk headscarf, and her silver studded earrings.

Yves wore knee-shorts, crew socks, deck shoes, and a comfortable burgundy hockey jersey.

They left Paris early, glad to get out of city traffic. At that hour, most of the traffic was coming into the city. They were for a while stuck in massive traffic on the peripheral highway that circles Paris. Once they were on the A4 heading east-northeast in the direction of Reims, Verdun, Metz, Thionville, it was straight shooting all the way. They stopped for lunch in a pizzeria in a small town near the Meuse River. They split a small pie topped with *peperoni*, mushroom, olives, and tomatoes. They washed it down with crackling Vichy water with a slice of lemon. They crossed the border amid grasslands and forests, marked with a square blue sign on the highway containing the word Luxembourg at the center of a standard EU circle of small stars. They zipped through what looked like a truck weighing station. It was much like crossing from one state to another in the USA, she thought. No more international checkpoints like in the old days when Dad was stationed in Europe. They were now in Luxembourg and cruising toward the capital city on European Route 25 (E-25).

ಬಿ • ಉ

"That was not so bad," Yves said cheerfully as they cruised into the *Gare* quarter, the main train station on the south side of the capital. The Gare was a large, antique-looking Belle Epoque building with weathered greenish-copper roofing on complex mansards and round windows and little turrets.

"Everything is so small and cute," she said.

He shrugged. "It's almost the tiniest big country in the world. Only places like Andorra, Liechtenstein, and the Vatican are smaller."

"And Monaco," she added for precision.

"There are a few," Yves allowed. He poked a finger at the GPS on the dash. The female voice speaking told them they were already close to their destination. They cruised along the Avenue de la Liberté, crossing the Grand-Duke Adolphe bridge over the Petrusse Valley with its tall cliffs and overhanging green tree crowns. There, visible across the valley, rose the thin spires of the national Notre Dame Cathedral, in this staunchly Catholic country, darkly (or brightly, depending on how you looked at it) dedicated to

Mary, Consoler of the Bereaved. European history, Hannah thought, had a lot to feel bereaved about. In ten minutes, they had circled the High or Old City and were in Limpertsberg.

"Wow, that was quick," Hannah said.

"There we are." They pulled into a driveway that was narrow, descending between mossy green stone walls overhung with ivy, down into a cobblestone quartier with a mix of old and surprisingly antiseptic looking new buildings (plain walls, straight sheet glass windows) designed to blend in.

Standing on the sidewalk, waving, was Rob. At his arm was a slender, shapely brunette with a quietly, smolderingly beautiful face. "That must be Elise," Hannah said delightedly. She waved, and Elise's face lit up with pleasure. "We're going to get along fine," Hannah said.

An older man stepped out, wearing gray trousers and a white dressy shirt missing a necktie. "I'll bet that is her papa," Yves said.

Papa guided Yves to a safe place to park, nosing into an impossibly tight looking corner overlooking the *Grund* valley through some bushes and trees.

They got out and made happy introductions. Hannah found that the Europeans usually did not warm up as quickly to strangers as North Americans or even the English would. Here, the ice was already broken because Rob and Elise clung inseparably to each other (which made Hannah happy to see).

It was early midafternoon by now, and the Gillen household smelled of fresh coffee and sweet cakes. Everyone but the English (tea drinkers) seemed to be coffee drinkers across Europe, Hannah observed, so she felt right at home as they sat around a sunny, airy living room table adjoining a large, modern kitchen. Elise's mother, a heavy-set, pleasant woman in her sixties, had prepared a generous *Kaffi* with ham, butter, bread, sweets, and that pungent coffee.

"We just ate in Verdun," Yves said apologetically. "We'll do our best."

Elise's parents laughed congenially. "The stuff won't run away. You can always eat a little later. You must be tired from your drive."

Yves said as he held a chair for Hannah and then took his own seat: "The hardest part was fighting our way out of rush hour traffic in Paris. After that, it was a picnic."

 ∛ • K

After refreshments, the Gillens took their guests out into the backyard to show them the view (green and pretty) of the valley with the tiny Petrusse stream flowing far below, and those granite cliffs that had once held gun emplacements in the age of gunpowder, knee breeches, and tri-cornered hats. Like most Luxemburgers, the Gillens were avid gardeners and planted flowers, hedges, and fruit trees in every available cranny. The house itself was stone, over two centuries old, with mossy streaks vertically flowing in generations of rainfalls over gray stucco.

"Yes," explained Professor Gillen, who taught Classics at the University of Luxembourg nearby. "Our family emigrated here during the Napoleonic era from Belgium. My ancestor was an engineer in the Department of Forests, as the French called this region before Napoléon Bonaparte was defeated, and everyone met in Vienna in 1815 to put Humpty Dumpty back together again. Our name meant something like 'waffles' in Flemish, so my ancestor assumed a more Luxembourgeois name, and we became *la famille* Gillen."

Elise, who had a dry sense of humor behind those shy, veiled eyes, said: "He was going to us the House of Luxembourg, but the name was already taken."

They all laughed, imagining the sorts of penalties one might suffer for usurping an aristocratic title back in the days when such things mattered far more than they did now. Papa explained that the House of Luxembourg had ceased to exist during the 1600s, and the current Grand Ducal family are most closely related to the House and Duchy of Nassau in Germany. Elise's father laughed and said: "I'm glad that we will never again be mistaken for waffles."

Banter continued in a light and congenial get-together. Elise's parents liked Hannah and her boyfriend, and Rob showed every sign of getting on okay with Yves, in a manly and fist-bumping manner.

In fact, as Hannah figured these things naturally and inevitably played out, Elise was already making signs of wanting to take Hannah window-shopping among some wonderful small but ritzy shops in the city, while Rob and Yves were hot on the topic of a scheduled Berlin-Vienna *Fussball* game, which Prof. Gillen offered to watch with them in a sports bar near the Place Guilleaume. That square, in the center of the Haute-Ville, was sort of your classical tree-lined, cobblestone square from any old European city, even complete with a small shop-lined *passage* at one end leading from the Guilleaume II Square to the Rue du Curé; typically Luxemburgish, probably the tiniest such passage anywhere in the world.

Hannah found that you had to get used to conversing in at least three languages for everyday affairs; like you could wish someone *guden Owend* (similar to German *guten Abend*) for good evening, but you could just as well use the French *bon soir*, and nobody would bat an eyelash. For good day, everyone said *bonjour*. You might say *muergen* for morning, or the similar-sounding *moien* for mid-day (as in French *moyen* meaning middle, she supposed). It was enough to make Hannah's head spin.

∾ ● ℭ

It was understood that Hannah and Rob needed time to examine their Dad's papers in the briefcase. They sat together alone in the dining room. Mme. Gillen cleared away used dishes, and served fresh coffee.

"Wow," Hannah said time and again as she picked up one familiar photograph or piece of paper after another.

"My first grade report card," Rob said at one point.

"My Girl Scout badges," Hannah said at another moment.

"Why do you suppose he labeled his journal with a Roman numeral three?" Rob asked.

Hannah shook her head. "Maybe there were two others before that, and we may find them or not."

Rob took a closer look at the opening pages of the notebook. "Looks like he just starts kind of abruptly here in the 1980s. But he seems to indicate he was continuing from a previous journal." He pointed at a smeared, inky scribble along the upper edge of the opening cardstock cover. "He says here ETS and then return to CONUS." He rapped himself on the forehead lightly with his knuckles as if that would shake his brain into thinking more clearly. "I think CONUS is a military expression for Continental United States. I've seen that in some books."

"What is ETS then?"

Rob slowly shook his head, mystified.

"We'll have to find that earlier journal," Hannah said. "Unless it's from that unhappy time of his life, and maybe he just burned it when he returned to the USA."

Rob slowly leaved through the pages. "The first part is sketchy. He doesn't go into detail about the weather or everything he did…"

She picked up from there: "…He packed thirty years of marriage into a 200-page notebook. That's not a diary. That's a record of major events. Like when they got married. When you and I were born."

Rob pointed. "You're right, but occasionally he does mention a major emotional milestone. Like here, in 1988 he first met Mom."

"We'll have kids one day," Hannah said, "and we'll want to pass this all along to them."

"And understand what it all means," Rob added.

Most of Journal III concerned the married years of Daniel and Nancy Wilson. They found a copy of her death certificate taped to a page near the end of the journal. "It ends with him dying," Rob said. "I have the death certificate, and I'll tape it in there on the last page, which will close out his Journal."

"A life well lived," Hannah said tenderly.

"Except for a mistake early on."

"We all make mistakes."

"I know, but he regretted something all his life. Something to do with that woman he married in Germany, and her family."

"Sounds like a huge, life-changing mistake whatever it was. I'll bet there are two missing journals and we'll find themone day," Hannah said. "Journal I and Journal II."

Together, they followed the chronology written in Dad's pressured, uneven blue ballpoint pen. Rob noted that Dad and Mom were both born in Oregon in 1950. They had never met until 1988.

In 1975, as the Vietnam War was ending, Dad finished college on a draft deferment, and joined the Army as a private even though he had nearly completed a Bachelor's in History. It was a sentimental journey of sorts, because Dan's father had been a career Army man. A mixed picture also, because Granddad had a reputation for having been a hard drinker, a fighter, and a stubborn man. Smart in some ways, thick as a brick in others. As Rob and Hannah looked closely, some of the blurred writing from long ago seemed to indicate there were two predecessor journals I and II. After a mixture of wonderful and terrible times while Dad was stationed in West Germany before his return 'back to the World' (as G.I.s called the United States). The terrible stuff had to be before 1980—including the death of a child, and a divorce—so Dan Wilson had returned to CONUS to start life over virtually from scratch. He had lost or given up everything in the process of separating from the service: a child, a wife, a career (the military, had he chosen to stay), a life (his friends, residence, village, everything of those five years), and so, a good part of his soul.

The German wife was a young woman of Croatian-German descent named Stana or Stanislava. The child that had died was their baby Klara (like the French name Claire). The inlaws hated Americans, and had given him a hard time. The driving force had been this drunken, raving ex-Croatian war criminal hiding in the mountains north of Heidelberg, with his corner blathering and mania (so Dan Wilson had briefly noted in an obscure footnote of his Journal III; no love lost). Except for that one outburst about Mischa Chetko, the father in law, Journal III did not mention Heidelberg directly again. Stana had stayed behind when he left to begin an entirely new life. That was all one could glean from his cursive scribbles.

Dan Wilson decompressed from his agony over the next decade, with some very limited counseling assistance from the Veterans Administration. By 1990, he had stabilized enough, after ten years back in CONUS, to meet, fall in love with, and marry Nancy. In 1990, the twins were born, who were now 30 in 2020. Nancy and Dan had a happy marriage 1990-2018, until Nancy died of leukemia in 2018, age 68. The last pages of the journal contained some odd, scratchy notes in a shaky hand. Last was Nancy's death certificate, and one more page blank, where Rob was now going to tape Dad's death certificate. Dad had died in his sleep, aged 70.

As they closed the journal together, and sat pensively regarding its enigmatic covers, Hannah said: "There is more to this story."

Rob smiled darkly. "Isn't that what Dad always said? There are other chapters yet to be written?"

She folded her hands and shook her head. "But he's gone. So the chapters maybe will be what happens in our lives next. That's the most logical explanation, right?" But she wasn't entirely convinced by her own explanation. But what else could it mean, unless it was nonsense? They rose and went to join the Gillen family in their pleasant activities. Rob, the Professor, and Yves walked up the cobblestone alley to a sports bar to watch the Berlin-Vienna game. Hannah and Elise walked with the boys as far as the sports bar, and then continued their walk in to the pleasant, quiet Old City with its shops and eateries, tree-lined squares and outdoor cafés. The page was about to turn, and the next chapter began to be written.

On a street corner nearby in Luxembourg stood an attractive golden-haired woman in dark sunglasses, with her hands in the pockets of her plum colored raincoat, watching. Though the air had turned gray, promising drizzle by evening, she had an odd sort of glow behind her. A light drizzle seemed not to bother her, nor did any droplets adhere to her.

5.   Trip to Heidelberg

They called it a pilgrimage. Rob and Hannah agreed they would take a trip to Heidelberg, where their father had been stationed during the 1970s.

Elise and Yves were welcome to come, but each was busy. Elise had a big accounting project to finish in Frankfurt for EU auditors. Yves was helping a new pop music band (with lots of money backing them) get started in Paris, and so he begged off.

That left the twins on their own, and they agreed to meet in beautiful Heidelberg, a romantic university town on the Neckar River in Germany.

Hannah took a very fast train (TGV) across northern France from the *Gare de l'Est* or East Station in Paris. The route was circuitous, but the train was so fast that her trip ended up being a three hour journey by way of Strasbourg. From there she traveled to Karlsruhe, and then on a more local train arrived at the western *Bahnhof* in Heidelberg.

Rob had driven south from Frankfurt, and awaited her on the station platform. He embraced her, gave her a swing around, and then they scampered arm in arm through the big, oddly plain, glassy box of the station and out onto the spacious square in front.

"I booked us a pair of singles at a nice little hotel in the suburbs," he told her. "Got a bargain deal."

"Always glad to hear that." She did her makeup, looking into the passenger side overhead mirror. "I could use a little lunch, a glass of wine, and a rest. It wasn't a long trip, but it's always so stressful."

"Go go go," he echoed. "We'll fix you right up, sis."

"It's so beautiful here." She sighed, looking around at the small town atmosphere, the surrounding green Hartz Mountains, and the peaceful olive-drab Neckar River as they crossed it on a roadway bridge.

"To think that Dad was stationed here for nearly six years. Two enlistments."

"So long ago."

"Yes," he said, "and just about all that's left of the U.S. military here today is museum stuff. We had hundreds of thousands of troops in West Germany for half a century. When the Soviet Union collapsed, and the

Warsaw Pact with it, we pulled out and put people and hardware into the Middle East after those 2001 attacks in New York City and Washington."

"East and West Germany became simply Germany after 1989." She combed her fingers through her hair. "I am asking myself what made us come here. Was it to just have a weekend together in a fabulous touristy university city with so much to see? Or did you want to spend time digging up the past?"

He shrugged lightly. "Both?"

She laughed. "Have your cake and eat it, huh?"

"Without Dad here, we wouldn't know where to start."

"I'll start with a hot bath."

"Sounds good. I'll have a beer in the dining room while you do that."

They followed the S-Bahn tracks out of the city center and into a peaceful, clean suburb called Kirchheim—appropriately named Church Home, if one translated literally. It was the quintessential small town German environment.

ʀ) • ß

The hotel room was quiet and clean, lit only by a faint glow from the street outside. That was the Heuauerweg, which literally meant sort of 'hay swamp road.' It was a very old street name, reflecting the fact that in previous centuries this had been farm country. Much of the land surrounding Heidelberg still today consisted of farmland divided into rectangular patches. Some of those acreages had been plowed and showed lines in the brown soil. Other acreages had been let go to seed, as farm acreage must to regenerate itself from exhaustion about one in five or seven years. All the signs of small town German and European life were here, from tram tracks on the street to nearby churches and a cemetery. Up the street were a modern supermarket, a tiny town hall, and a school.

As Hannah showered, enjoying a nice steamy relief after traveling, and as Rob sat over a cool, tangy Bitburg Pils at a heavy oak table in the Hotel Heidelberg's cozy *Stube* (parlor), a shadow moved across Hannah's empty little single room. It was a shadow resembling that of a woman—slender, moving in elegant and continuous motions almost as if to soft music like Claude Debussy's *Claire de Lune* (Moonlight)—who swept through Rob's room, passed through the wall like a ghost or a messenger or an angel and into Hannah's room, where she pulled her delicate, long-fingered hand through the air after her, ballet-like, leaving a small object fluttering in the still air before she faded away through the opposite wall.

ʀ) • ß

Hannah emerged from the steamy bathroom, toweling herself and humming brightly. It was dim in the room, and she flicked a wall switch.

Something was different in the room, but she couldn't immediately tell what it was. She toweled herself, sat and used the hairdryer that blew noisily in her ear, shut that off, and sorted through her fresh clothes. As she sat on the bed, slipping her briefs on, she noticed a white rectangle. Picking it up, she read: *Peter Towns, U.S. Army (Ret.), Tour Guide (English and German spoken). Forty years in Heidelberg—I know my way around and want to make your stay complete with an expert guided tour.*

Odd. How had this gotten here? It didn't surprise her. Maybe the hotel got a kickback for promoting his tours. She'd lived in Europe long enough to have seen many such cooperative schemes to milk tourists; but often the tourists benefited from good services, as did those who brokered shops and services or provided them. She finished dressing, applied light makeup, brushed her hair, tucked the card in her pocket, picked up her purse, and headed out the door to find Rob.

ⅎ ● ℸ

Rob was in the *Stube* downstairs, sipping a second beer. "Hey, sis."

She asked fondly: "How are you?"

"Buzzed. Feeling good. Have a beer."

"Don't mind if I do." She slid into the chair opposite him at his big oak table. A red candle burned in a glass receptacle amid tomorrow's napkins, plates, and dinnerware. The staff were getting ready for next morning's buffet for the thirty or more tourists staying in the hotel.

"Look what I found." She showed him the card.

"A-hah. Well, if it's legit, we might just have ourselves a fun tour. Hold on." He rose, took the card, and went to the ornate wooden front desk cubicle. There, he spoke for a few minutes with a young blonde receptionist with thick black glasses and violet lipstick. She nodded a lot and looked efficient.

Rob returned. "It's on. This guy Peter Towns is known here in the hotel. He has given tours before."

She checked her watch. "Eight o'clock. Suppose there is still time to call him today?"

Rob nodded. "Try it. He'll want the business."

Hannah rang him, using a local cell exchange.

"Yes?" A man with an older-sounding voice answered.

"Mr. Towns, I'm sorry to bother you so late. My brother and I are at the hotel, and wondered if we could arrange a tour with you."

"I'd love to help. When did you have in mind?"

"We're here for a three day weekend. How about tomorrow?"

"As good as done."

With a little more conversation, she had a reasonable price lined up for a four hour tour that would include the picturesque Old Town with its popular main shopping street, and the parallel street that ran along the Neckar shore, lined with university buildings, an old synagogue restored after the war, and other sights worth seeing. The other half of the tour would take them up to the castle on the hill.

℘ • ℭ

Peter Towns met them at the main trolley station downtown. He was a stocky, powerful looking man of about 65, Dad's generation, with wavy white hair and a florid face. He wore a dark blue sweater with white shirt collars protruding; and khaki pants with good brown walking shoes. He shook hands with both as Rob and Hannah introduced themselves.

As they began walking, he told them a little bit about his career, first in Vietnam as a combat infantry soldier wounded twice in the legs but lucky to survive; and then as an administrative NCO, stationed in San Francisco, Washington, D.C., and finally the last twelve years in Heidelberg. "I'm still married to a German girl after all these years. We have three kids now in their twenties who are more German than they are American, and everyone is happy."

They walked down the picturesque main street in the university quarter, which was lined for a good quarter mile with bars, shops, restaurants, a church or two, and a number of university clinics and office buildings. "This is one of the best tourist cities in Europe," he told them. "I've seen them all, from Rome to Berlin, Prague to Budapest, and Vienna and Nuernberg and so on. Heidelberg is compact, only 150,000 or so residents, and still a small town while hosting a world-class university."

During their walk, with hundreds of tourists, locals, and students circulating around them, Rob mentioned their dad. "You're an old soldier retired and living in Heidelberg, sir. Our dad was stationed here many years ago."

"What was his name and unit?"

"Dan Wilson, junior enlisted guy, basically worked as a file clerk and rose to office manager, I think that's E-5 just a grade shy of NCO at E-6. Do I have that right?"

Towns' red, grizzled face lit up in a grin. "That's the Army for you. They always dangled the next promotion before your eyes, to get you to re-up. He probably made E-5 specialist just after reenlisting. That's soft stripe; the hard stripe would be sergeant or buck sergeant as they call it. If he behaved himself and had a good record, he would probably have been on the E-6 list for Staff Sergeant right after reenlisting. What did he decide to do?"

Hannah said: "He had a real hard time. Bad marriage, baby that died, superiors who weren't very supportive; and inlaws who hated him. Being peasants in a remote village, they hated anyone outside or different, including the 'crazy Americans' as we are known around the world."

Towns' face contracted. "Sounds like he had a run of bad luck. Everyone goes through at least one streak of that in the military. Everyone has the Boss from Hell at some point in his or her career. You just duck down, keep your mouth shut, and endure it."

"Misery has company, eh?" Rob said.

Towns nodded. "For sure. I had my BFH during my one tour back in CONUS. I was just past my twenty, and almost separated out of the Army."

"Oh!" Hannah interrupted, remembering... "What is ETS?"

Towns said: "ETS meant Estimated Time of Separation. For junior enlisted folks, that was the day they counted down to, their liberation. Their emancipation from the hell they saw as being in the military. They were fools, because they had three hots and a cot here, a dream, and they could travel all over Europe at will. I used to love driving down to Paris, or over to Brussels, and sometimes Vienna or Berlin. So ETS was your liberation date."

"Why estimated," Rob asked. "Couldn't they give you a firm date?"

"Oh no," Towns said with gruff heartiness. "Not the Army. You've heard the expression that there's the right way, the wrong way, and the Army way? Well, when you are in the Army, everything you do is 'at the convenience of the service.' If they needed you to extend a couple of months, it was wide open. It never really happened that I know of, but it would have killed these junior enlisted people who were really still kids at age twenty or twenty-one. Every one of them had a short timer's calendar with a picture on it, divided into a bunch of little numbered squares. It might be a boot, a hat, or a doorway. Whatever. They'd have a crayon handy, and every day color in another square counting downward to day zero—their ETS."

Hannah and Rob nodded. "So that explains Dad's notes about ETS."

Towns nodded. "Separation from the service, and return to CONUS. Actually, if you chose to get out, your last day would occur someplace back in the Continental United States like Fort Dix."

"Did you keep a short-timer's calendar in your first enlistment?" Hannah asked.

Towns said: "And how. Every one of us did."

"And you changed your mind."

He grinned. "I had three hots and a cot that a tourist would pay tens of thousands of dollars for. I had girlfriends in three different cities—one in Heidelberg, one in Frankfurt, and one in Stuttgart. Hell, I tore up that stupid calendar and realized I had it made. I still had a lot of the world to see, so why return home and be a pig farmer for the rest of my life in Nebraska?"

Hannah sighed deeply. "I was never in the service, but I see what you mean. I work for a company in Paris, and my brother works for one in Frankfurt."

"Think about it," Towns said. "Lots of U.S. military and civil service retired here. We have universal health care and all sorts of social nets in all these countries, unlike the USA. We're still living in the dark ages over there, pretending health care is some sort of evil communism. It's every man for himself, while the medical corporations rake in zillions of our dollars. It's a ridiculous brainwash... but don't get me going."

"Is there any way to find out more about where our Dad worked, what he did, where he lived, that sort of thing?"

"When was this?"

"In the 1970s. He returned home in 1981."

Towns shook his head. "I've been here since 1980. Not sure our paths ever crossed. But I'll tell you what. There are some clubs here, nostalgia things, you know? A lot of us have fond memories of when this whole part of Germany was crawling with U.S. and Allied service people and civilians. We got along pretty well with the Germans, with the usual few exceptions here and there."

Verlorenau, said a voice in Hannah's head. She spoke up. "I just remembered something. I think he mentioned once that he lived in a village up in the mountains, by the name of Verlorenau.

"I just remembered the same thing," Rob said. It was almost as if a ghostly voice had whispered in his inner ear.

"That gives me something to work with," Towns said. "I'll tell you what. I'll be happy to do a little research for you at no charge. Always glad to help out an old comrade, even if he's gone and I'm helping his children."

"Oh that would be so wonderful," Hannah said.

"Thank you," Rob chimed in.

ೞ • ೮ౠ

They made a detour along the river, saw the bridge where so many famous people had walked over the centuries, and the Philosophers' Walk across the river in the forest. Just beyond the university end of the city, modern-looking castle ruins stood so beautifully and tragically on the hills above. Towns related a lot of information he'd gleaned over the years.

The university, founded just before 1400, played a central role in the destructive wars of religion that racked Europe for at least two centuries. Martin Luther, the German priest who launched the Reformation, came here in 1518 after proclaiming his 95 Theses against the existing Church in 1517.

The upper castle was destroyed in a gunpowder explosion in 1537, but the lower palace served as a ducal stronghold until it, too, was demolished in a series of wars about the usual struggles for power and wealth, using the peasants as cannon fodder, typically sending thousands upon thousands of villagers and commoners to their deaths on some pretense related to religion (the Protestant-Catholic divide being a volatile and rich source of combustible energy for that purpose).

Ultimately, it was always a power grab by one oligarchic or aristocratic (same thing; just different funny hats) faction against another. Rob, the political philosopher, had a field day discussing these matters with Towns, who had no reason to disagree. He had served in a lost cause of his own, the Vietnam War, for which he could offer no more logical explanation than for the beautiful carcass of history lying on the hilltops above Heidelberg.

Peter Towns left the siblings on excellent terms around four p.m., with instructions to explore the picturesque main street with its many shops, restaurants, and bars as evening fell and nightlife began.

As Rob and Hannah were having a traditional dinner of Bratwurst, Sauerkraut, and potato dumplings in a tangy beef sauce, Hannah's phone warbled and she answered.

It was Towns. "I found something for you. I hope this helps. There is a retired sergeant major by the name of Jack Rinconi, used to work as a records honcho in Schwetzingen. That's a town nearby where we had theater-level personnel services and actions. If you were stationed in USAREUR, chances were good that your file at some point passed through Schwetzingen. Rinconi lives in a little village called Ödendorf just down the road and downhill from Verlorenau. I can hook you up with him, and that's about the best I think I can do."

"That's wonderful," Hannah said over the phone and over the din of voices and diners in the crowded little *Gaststätte* (roughly, 'guest place').

6.   Village Cemetery

In the morning, Rob and Hannah drove up into the hills northeast of Heidelberg, in the direction of Peterstal (Peter's Valley) but beyond. The narrow country road took them ever higher into dense forest among hilltops and low mountains, until they came to a crossroads with an ancient stone fountain. The fountain was topped with a stone Keltic cross covered with dark green moss and whitish lichens. Among the massive tree crowns, they could make out red rooftops all around. A sign read: *Ödendorf.*

An older, olive-skinned man stood waiting for them. He was white haired, and looked to be a robust, strapping seventy or seventy-five. He recognized Rob's Frankfurt license plate (F followed by numbers) and raised a hand in relaxed greeting. When they got out, he introduced himself as Jack Rinconi.

"Thank you for meeting with us," Hannah said.

"My pleasure. This is on the house. No charge. Always glad to help a deceased veteran's kids."

They shook hands and stood admiring the sunny, breezy heights.

"You can almost see Heidelberg Castle from here on a really clear day," Jack Rinconi told them. He was from New York State, but had now lived in Germany as long as he'd spent during his youth in USA.

Hannah said: "We're from Oregon, but we live in Europe." They explained their current occupations.

"Wonderful," Jack said. "Why don't you park, and I'll drive. I know my way around here."

Towns left his vehicle in a small lot near the fountain. They all clambered into his Volkswagen bus, which had six or eight interior seats that made it not a van.

Jack drove along a one-lane mountain lane. "We're almost on private land here," he explained as the road became bumpier. It looked almost like one of those ancient Roman post roads that are all over Europe. Sharp bluish rocks stuck out of hard clay earth, with moss on the stone surfaces. They rolled into the final village on this mountain loop, where Dad had lived with his first wife for several years.

Ᏸ • Ꮳ

A stone marker proclaimed in Germanic lettering, which looked as if it came from Kaiser times a century or more ago: *Verlorenau*.

"This is as far out as you go in the Heidelberg area. Your dad married someone up here?"

Rob said: "We think her name was Stana."

"Sounds Eastern European," Jack said. "Something immediately suspicious there. Last name?"

"We think it was Chetko."

"Hmm. That's definitely not German. Stana would be short for Stanislava, which could be Russian or Stanislawa, Polish... lots of possibilities. Something strange there." Jack got a concerned look as he drove slowly, with his hands resting loose and relaxed on the wheel. At one point, he had to pull aside to let a late model VW Golf race past.

"What do you mean?" Rob asked.

"Well, it's a generation before my time at least. The old Germans used to talk about it. At the end of World War Two, this part of Europe had the largest refugee crisis in history. About thirty million people uprooted, including people of German heritage fleeing Slavic areas they'd lived in for hundreds of years. Millions of refugees were Eastern European slave laborers who had to be housed, fed, and repatriated."

"Slave labor?" Rob asked incredulously.

"Sure. The Nazis had their own young men away fighting, and the women worked in factories or drove the busses or whatever. So they brought in lots of Eastern Europeans as farm slaves and factory slaves."

"Hitler was just making Germany great again," Hannah said with bitter sarcasm. "And turned all of Europe into a charnel house."

"As did Napoleon Bonaparte," Rob echoed their earlier conversations with Steve Towns. "Human nature never changes."

Hannah said: "Why do humans have to get so ugly?"

"Power," Jack said. "Greed. Money. Every generation has its megalomaniacs, and their simple, stupid followers. The uneducated who can't think for themselves just love all that brutality; it makes them feel powerful themselves. Anyway, there was this huge flood of refugees. Among them, hiding, were tens of thousands of war criminals fleeing from justice. Everything from KZ supervisors to SS murderers and Gestapo types. A lot from the Balkans and that area also."

"I hope that part of history never repeats itself," Rob said.

Jack said: "Oh, but I think it does. As soon as people forget the horrors of the past, they start all over again. Another demagogue comes along and stirs up the lower half with false info and vague threats. Then the bankers and industrialists and generals see their opportunities, as they did when Hitler came to power in Germany, or Mussolini in Italy. They thought they could control him, but that kind of guy is like fire on gasoline with his hordes of uninformed, unthinking rabble. Then those hordes get put in uniforms and sent off to war to die for the moneyed class. They're told it's for Jesus or the homeland, and they fanatically believe all the lies. It's an ancient story, in our DNA, and it's going to forever cycle in a loop. Oops, there she be."

"Be who?" Rob mimicked.

"Where I want to start. The village cemetery."

ℬ • ℭ

Verlorenau was a settlement of neat, sturdy looking stone houses that had to withstand extra winds and cold up here in the snowy winters, even though the Heidelberg climate itself was among the mildest in Germany.

The uphill road led into a little village square, actually a circle, with a statue in the center. The statue, which serviced a fountain as did the Keltic cross in Jack's village further down the winding mountain lane, was of a man in a military coat, looking heroic as all such statues must. Whoever he was, he was a man of the 1800s, with a full beard and long hair hanging over a wide collar, or so he had been hewn from granite. Another sign read *Bevölkerung* (Population): 350 *anno* 2000 N.C. (*nach Christus*, after Christ, like A.D.). So in 2000, about 350 persons had been permanent residents. Probably had not changed significantly in the past twenty years. Looking at the sign, Jack said philosophically: "In a few years, that will be a quarter century ago. That's how time flies. As an old retired Army NCO, with my wife terminally ill with cancer, I'm acutely conscious of such things." He added: "Mortality. We've already made arrangements to be buried in *Ödendorf.* My wife is German. She was born there, and we met in Heidelberg where she worked as a secretary for our general staff." He sighed. "It's been a good life. I have nothing to complain about."

The lane made a circle around the fountain and statue. At the edges were several small buildings. These included a squat stone church (Evangelical, meaning Lutheran), Kindergarten (literally a children's garden), a little - grammar school, a tiny one-room library, and a modern, glassy one-story *Rathaus* or town hall. As Jack explained, *der Rat* meant council, not rodent, which would be *die Ratte* and pronounced differently. "I have to explain this stuff endlessly to Amis," he said, meaning Americans. "This little village square branches out in five different directions, like a star. Each direction has a little road leading out to a settlement of farms. At the end of the main one is the old Forsthaus, the lodge of the forest master or *Waldmeister*. That's the most prestigious local office here. The Germans still worship trees, although they've destroyed most of them through acid rain, and Hitler used them for the war industry. Harming a tree will get you a severe penalty under German law."

"We love trees," Rob said.

"We hug them all the time."

"You have a lot of them up there in Oregon, huh? We do too, in upstate New York."

"You're going to make me homesick all of a sudden," Hannah said. A tear formed in one eye as she thought of her parents and the recent funeral, which was still fresh in her dreams and memories.

Jack had no idea, and carried on happily. "I used to come up here twice a week evenings for beer and cards with a bunch of Germans. They have a really nice Gaststatte up here called *Zum Forst*, which means something like At the Forest. But let's check out the cemetery first." He pulled around under a weeping willow by a clean new stone wall and they got out.

The parking area was graveled and well-tended, strewn with willow debris. "One piece of bad news," Jack said, as he stretched his rangy frame. "They clean out the cemeteries every twenty-eight years. People either pay to renew for another twenty-eight years, or their gravestone is handed to a stonebreaker to be made in to gravel."

"Ouch," Rob said. "Sounds kind of cold-blooded, eh? Dad left here in 1980, which is now forty years ago."

"Well," Jack said sadly, "if nobody renewed the mortgage, so to speak, there will be no stone. They don't dig up the dead but usually leave them in place. In fifty or a hundred years when a new burial takes place at that spot, about all you'll find is a skull at best."

"How cheerful," Hannah said drily.

They walked through a wooden gate of two swinging halves, and entered what looked like a small garden of high hedges, wild blue amarys and other flowering plants, and tilted, broken, mossy stones. "The real old ones are left in place," Jack explained. "They refer to everywhere long ago, meaning before Nazi times, as the Old People. That includes everyone from the Old Stone Age forward." He enumerated: "Indigenous, Keltic or Gaulish, Germanic which means mostly Frankish, Romans who had a huge presence all over Europe, then the Goths and Franks and other invaders, and finally the Medieval, Renaissance, and Modern people. And, as you have probably noticed, Europe is covered with ruins from so many wars between Protestant and Catholic warlords after 1500. Tyrants, all the same. Our magic is better than your magic, so we have to kill you all."

They walked into a small building, whose single door admitted them to a little hall dimly illumined by plain yellowish leaded glass windows in steel frames. It was chilly in here, and smelled vaguely of flowers and chemicals.

The atmosphere gave Hannah the creeps. It inspired a mixture of reverence and downright fear.

"There is probably an official register in here," Jack said. "Ah, look on the wall." There, painted in a dark red brush-script in antique script, were lists of names and birth-death dates. The script was neither traditional Germanic nor modern, but a sort of flowing, artistic imitation of Medieval illumined cursive. Jack concluded: "Past inhabitants of this village."

The three of them looked, but could find no Chetko.

"There is a Stanislava," Jack said, pointing.

"Oh, my, god," Hannah intoned. She read out loud: "Stanislava Bautz-Chetko, 1955-2015 . She was about sixty when she died just a few years ago."

How sad this all is, Hannah thought. "No wonder Dad was a wreck."

"I'm feeling like a wreck right now too," Rob whispered.

Jack spoke quietly. "She died relatively young. Must have been cancer. Suicide. Who knows. We'll find out more. I'm curious now." He traced a finger up and down the list of villagers' names, which dated as far back as 1920. "There are probably people buried on this hill dating back thousands of years," Jack said. "This is just modern cemetery lore from the post-World War Two recovery. A new world. Look." He found another name with Bautz in it. "Anna Maria Bautz-Chetko, 1925 to 1995. I'll lay odds that is the mother of this Stana. So where is her husband, Klara's father?"

They searched the wall of names in vain. No sign of a Chetko with probably an Eastern European first name. "We'll try the tavern next," Jack said. Then his features lit up. "Look. There is another name under Stanislava's. I almost missed it." He ran a fingertip along a faint, indented name in smaller print. "Klara Bautz-Chetko W. I would guess that the initial stand for Wilson."

Hannah felt faint. Rob grabbed her elbow to support her, as well as steady himself.

"Our little sister," Hannah whispered. Klara's dates were given as simply one year, 1979.

"We weren't born yet," Rob whispered, and his voice echoed faintly in that cold chamber.

Jack shook his head gravely, amazed at the meanspiritedness. "They wouldn't even allow your father's name in here. They must have really hated him. But that was the baby's name. Klara Wilson, when you get right down to the unalterable facts."

"Claire Wilson," Hannah whispered, and her voice echoed aroud her.

ଞ • ଘ

When they stepped back into the cemetery outside, the light had grown a bit darker, more somber. A wind blew, throwing around shreds and fragments of last autumn's dead leaves.

Jack waited by the gate, while Rob and Hannah made a tour of the small cemetery. The center had been denuded of gravestones, leaving only rows of tall weeds where the graves still lay in their low, crumbling dark stone borders grown over with moss. The place could have stood empty for centuries as far as maintenance was concerned, or the strange absence of maintenance. It was almost as if the villagers in their neat houses did not want to come here, except to bury each other, and then quickly leave back to their normal living, breathing, blood-pumping days of light and conversation.

Hannah plucked at Rob's sleeve. "I could swear I feel eyes on us."

He nodded. "Maybe someone noticed us coming up here, and decided to keep an eye on us strangers."

Hannah looked around. "But who, and where? I don't see anyone."

"All gone," Jack said from afar. "Nobody paid the fee, and the markers went to the stone breakers down in the valley." He was beginning to seem uneasy and impatient. "Come on, let's go Zum Forst."

They stepped out through the gate, glad to be back in the world of the living.

The sunlight appeared brighter and softer, the air warmer, the light wind balmy. No leaves blowing around.

As they headed back to Jack's van, he said: "I saw someone watching us from far away in the trees. A woman with sunglasses. A bit odd, I'd say. Didn't say anything, no facial expression, just kept her hands in the pockets of her raincoat and stared our way from behind those black shades. Seemed to have a faint glow behind her, but I am sure I was seeing things."

Nobody said it, but the thought hung in the air, as memories sometimes do, floating smoke not anchored either to heaven or earth:

Claire Wilson.

7.   Village Tavern *Zum Forst*

Jack drove slowly, with the sureness of someone who had been here many times. The narrow little village road took them around the central monument again, and out along a street labeled *Eichengasse,* or Oaktree Alley. "Each of the main alleys has a tree name," Jack explained.

They pulled up in a miniature parking lot suitable for a dozen cars at most. Beyond it, snug in the forest, was Zum Forst. It was as picturesque a building as Hannah could imagine.

"Built around 1870," Jack said as he pulled the brake tight and opened his door. "I know because the owner told me. I used to come here to drink beer and play cards before that whole generation died out, or most of them did. There is one old-timer left, and I hope we can talk with him."

They trooped into the small restaurant, where it seemed the whole village was assembled for the noon meal. The air smelled richly of meat, gravy, potatoes, and pickled cabbage.

"You guys hungry?" Jack asked.

"Now that you mention it," Rob said.

"Starving," Hannah said.

An attractive middle-aged woman with slightly lined features brought them leather-bound menus. *Guten Tag, meine Freunde.* "Good day, my friends."

Danke; Gleichfalls, Jack said. "Thanks, same to you."

The woman wore tasteful, modern clothing as if she lived in the big city. Only a few men at adjoining tables wore corduroy or leather knee-breeches or culottes common in the region, along with high woollen stockings; some wore suspenders. Other than that, no yodeling or tourist scams, although Lederhosen shorts could still be a stock men's clothing item in Bavaria, way over near Austria and Switzerland. It seemed however that every German man around here was born wearing a dark green felt hat with a small feather in the band, a tribute to the respect with which the *Forstmeister* were held. It was, Rob said to Hannah at some point, the cowboy hat of Germans.

In another sign of modernity, there was a prominent sign: *Rauchen Verboten.* Smoking Prohibited.

"In my day, this place used to be thick with cigarette smoke," Jack said as he studied the menu. At his recommendation, they tried a hot, steaming dish of crispy potato pancakes with salt and sour cream, along with piquant Bratwurst in sharp mustard. To stay sharp, they decided instead of beer to order black coffee.

As they finished lunch, and waited for dessert in the form of small fruit tortes soaked in whipped cream and raspberry sauce, the proprietress, a Frau Hagel, returned from a brief trip down the road. With her came an elderly woman in a sweater and rumpled grayish house dress along with shoes that looked more like dark-green corduroy slippers. She was introduced as Frau Jones, and needed help climbing into a bench at the table. She was about 85, and partially blind, as her upturned filmy gray-blue eye in a pasty yellowish face attested. Her other eye was sharp as binoculars and looked straight into a person. She wore a plain dark blue scarf, loosely knotted under the chin, and wrapped around her gray-haired head. Not surprisingly, given her name that said much, she spoke excellent English with a mild German accent. "Welcome to our metropolis here in the mountains."

They all laughed and shook hands. She might not have both eyes, but her insight was clear. "I was married to a U.S. Army sergeant for over thirty years. His name was Tommy Johnson, and he was from Michigan. I was born in 1935, and I was just eighteen in 1953 when Tommy swept me off my feet. My parents didn't care for Americans that much, but they felt there was no future with our own Germans at that time. I had a brother killed in Russia, you see, only eighteen in 1944 when he disappeared near Stalingrad, so my parents had much grief, but so did all the German people. That defined our world, you see. What a lot of fools to listen to that insane barking dog from Austria." She shook her head, changing to a gentler mode. "Life with Tommy was good. We lived near Detroit for a time, but he reenlisted and we came back here to Germany, where he retired. He passed away in 1998. He was 69 and could have lived longer, but he smoked too much, and died of lung cancer." She was chatty, the old woman, which Hannah found helpful and informative.

Rob asked: "What do you know of a woman named Bautz? Anna Maria Bautz?"

"A cow," Mrs. Jones said sharply. "Bautz is a word for a cow. She was a cow, although a pretty one in her younger years. She just passed away not long ago."

"And a man named Chetko?"

"Oh that swine," she said darkly. She looked around, as if afraid to be overheard. "He is dead also, and the village refused to bury him here. So he was cremated and his ashes were eventually dumped in the river. Should have been the toilet." She whispered: "We found out he was a war criminal. He wanted to emigrate to the United States to continue his dirty work, I suppose, but the Americans were clever enough to spot a former *Ustashe*. So he was stuck here, and managed to grab Anna Maria Moo-Cow for a wife. And what a fiasco that was."

"What's an Ustashe?" Rob asked.

"Those were the worst of the worst, the Croatian fascists who made our German Nazis look mild."

"And Chetko was one of them?"

"Oh, of course." She nodded, making what Hannah called the European *poof-poof*, an exaggerated expression involving the entire upper body, from shaking the head 'no' while poofing the lips, to a sort of rolling shoulder shrug, which described something too absurd for words. "It all came out in the end. He pretended to be a refugee, when in fact he was implicated in mass murders. The European Court could never quite pin anything down, but people here put two and two together. He and his fellow terrorists in Belgrade would get drunk and go out looking for Jews or Gypsies or anyone else they hated. Then they would hold them down and saw their heads off with a hand-saw while the victims were screaming. Even the SS would turn pale when they saw that sorts of things that Chetko and his type did." She added: "What human beings aren't capable of." She changed the subject: "So who are you two fine young people?"

Hannah explained the nature of their mission, and their relationship with their guide, Jack. "Our father was Dan Wilson, who apparently married a Stana Chetko."

At this, the woman turned even paler, and her one good eye radiated horror. "Not Stanislava."

"Yes," Jack said. "Stana. Her name is on the wall in the mortuary."

Frau Jones nodded. "What a tragic family. And your poor father, to stumble into such a nest of vipers."

"What do you mean?"

Frau Jones appeared unable to speak, but just shook her head. "Such things. The war was awful enough, but such things."

Rob prodded: "Frau Jones, we came a long way. We hope you can be so kind and help us find answers. We want to know what happened to our father while he was stationed here."

The proprietress, Frau Hagel, came and sat beside her elderly friend. Apparently, Hagel's mother, now deceased, and Frau Jones had been best of friends in school, both in the Kindergarten and lower schools in *Verlorenau* and *Ödendorf*, as well as high school further down the valley near Heidelberg. That would have been during the Hitler years—long long ago.

Comforted by the closeness of her friend's daughter, Frau Jones continued, reluctantly, and in horrified whispers. "What I know, I learned from sources in the U.S. Army headquarters. They knew everything about the local Nazis and other war criminals. You couldn't jail or execute a quarter or more of the German population who ran behind Hitler and his henchmen. Most were stupid followers, as these people always are, just like today—so they lost interest and became almost normal people again after the little clown from Austria killed himself. Our entire world here was in ruins back in 1945. Just soldiers alone, Germany lost millions of young men for nothing, plus countless innocents everywhere who died. It can happen anywhere." She gave them a hard look (*Amerika heute…*).

Rob said: "Modern craziness aside, we had a civil war that cost nearly a million lives, for all the wrong reasons."

"You see," Frau Jones said. "Humans still live in trees."

Hannah nodded: "I live in Paris. There is enough evidence from French history to support what you're saying."

"Human history everywhere," Rob said, "including ours in the USA."

"And of course nobody wants to hear it about themselves, just about others." Frau Jones leaned close and whispered, so nobody else would hear. "Mischa Chetko was a monster. An alcoholic with delusions of grandeur, and a huge mean streak. He was a fanatic when he joined Ustasha, as Hitler invaded Croatia. I knew your father Danny, children."

"No," Rob and Hannah said in one breath.

"Pay dirt," Jack said happily, though with a reserve owing to the dark subjects under discussion.

"Dan Wilson was a good man." Frau Jones leaned ever closer, folding her hands on the checkered table cloth around Hannah's hands. "Child, Danny used to come in here and drink beer in the evenings. He looked so sad, and he drank too much, but nothing like Chetko. That was during the 1970s, when your father was younger than you are now. He was such a decent, devoted young man." Suddenly she brightened, pursuing a different train of thought in her aged and overflowing memories. She turned to Frau Hagel. "Irma, would you do something for me?"

Ja, Tante, was denn? "Yes, Aunt. What then?"

Frau Jones spoke in fast, thick German, the local dialect that was hard to follow if you only knew a little High German or *Hochdeutsch* as Rob did. Hannah was at a loss. Everyone in a village like this was either *Tante* or *Onkel*, Uncle. The kids went to school together, and played in a roving band on the hills, in the woods, on the village streets, preparing to be the next generation of villager owners.

Ja, ja, Frau Hagel said as Frau Jones handed her a house key. Irma Hagel rose and left quickly.

"She will bring you something very surprising," Frau Jones told the twins. "So in the meantime, my old eyes tell me maybe you are twins, eh?"

"Fraternal," Rob and Hannah said in one breath.

Hannah opened her purse and took out a few snapshots. Rob did the same with his wallet. They sat and gurgled happily together over pictures of Dan and Nancy, of the twins when they were young, and the house in Salem with the lantern by the ivied entrance.

"How delightful," Frau Jones said. "I am so glad to hear that Danny married again, to your beautiful mother, yes?"

They nodded. Hannah anticipated the next question. "They were very happy together for over thirty years. Mom's name was Nancy Everol, from Oregon."

"The U.S. state," said Frau Jones.

"Yes. We are from the Portland area."

"I love your country."

"Thank you. We love yours too."

"You must tell me all about your Dad, and his wives, including your mother, and about yourselves. I am so happy that everything turned out well for him. He was so sad when he lived her with Stana, and so young for so much tragedy. But we older Germans lived with terrible tragedy too, as did too many others. No making excuses but suffering is suffering. My brother died. I still miss him and love him today. He was just an ordinary boy, working as a *Kellner*, a waiter in this restaurant here for our parents, when they took him away to the Wehrmacht and he disappeared in Russia. We were rid of Hitler and his magpies, but that evil Chetko, he brought a special hell with him from Croatia."

Rob and Hannah spent the next fifteen minutes telling the elderly woman all about themselves, their state of Oregon, and their current lives in Europe.

"Your dad Danny would be so proud of you both," she said.

The door opened, and Irma Hagel walked in carrying the key—and a notebook. She slid in to the bench again beside Frau Jones, and handed her both objects.

Danke, Frau Jones said. *Gut geschafft*. "Thanks. Well done." She placed both hands palms down on the notebook. "This belonged to your father."

Hannah was stunned. What lay on the table before her was a notebook identical to that which her father had labeled Journal III. She bet that this one had an earlier number. She reached for it, and Frau Jones pushed it across the table to her. Peeking inside for a second, Hannah saw in the opening cover that her father had written the words Journal II. Rob leaned close to study it as well.

"This is yours now, children. I gladly hand it over to you. I feel I have waited forty years for this moment." Frau Jones briefly cried. Then she began to explain as much as she knew, which was a lot, but not all of the story.

Part Two

Journal II
Bridge of Regret

Paris and Heidelberg 1978-1980

8.　Another Piece of the Puzzle

"Terrible things happened in that family," Frau Jones said. "You must prepare yourselves when I tell you, because you will see what they all suffered when that monster came here. Driven by Chetko who was relentless—a drunkard, a loudmouth, a boisterous and boastful dirty man, and an extremely sly, intelligent or cunning one—they never totally confronted their tragedy." She paused, as if not sure she wanted to continue. Her lower lip trembled at the verge of again crying.

"Chetko was a bully and a braggard, always with his chin up and his mouth open, challenging anyone into his arguments, and those dirty little pig eyes of his cold as ice while he made grandiose declarations, gesturing a brutal finger in knife stabs. He was born a bully, was a fascist all his life, and died a bully without ever experiencing a moment of regret."

Hannah shook her head. "Sounds like a sociopath. Please, start at the beginning. How did our Dad ever get involved with this outfit?"

"Well," Frau Jones said, "love is blind. Look at me. I am almost blind, but this is not love. It is old age. I have tried reading your father's journal, which he forgot here one day. He was writing in it, and was drinking a bit too much beer—so sad, the poor boy—and he forgot his journal when he walked out that door for the last time. That would have been, what, forty years ago now. I was in my forties then, a young woman like Irma here."

Irma beamed, and called for two young waiters—her sons Hannah guessed—to bring more coffee and sweets. The lunch crowd was thinning out as men and women returned to their houses or farms or drove back down the hill to the office buildings in the valley around Ziegelhausen.

"The Bautz family lost a son in the war, as many of us did. They had two daughters and a surviving son, all of whom lived until the 2000s. One of the daughters was Anna Maria, the only one who stayed with her parents here in the village. The others moved to Heidelberg, married, and lived their lives out in the modern world. Anna Maria was a simple, quiet girl—a cow, I tell you—who stayed at home. And then this treacherous, boastful animal came here as a war refugee. What nobody realized was that he was a war criminal in hiding. One of the village girls, Fräulein Matthias, now also dead, told me long ago that she was doing some house cleaning for Anna Maria, when she saw a photo album on the coffee table in their livingroom. That is, the living room of Mischa Chetko and Stana, where Anna Maria lived when she got older. She peeked into the photo album out of curiosity, and there was Chetko decked out in some sort of dark uniform with medals and death's heads like the SS. He was a member of the Ustashe, the Croatian fascist terror regime that was worse than the Nazis. If you remember the horrible things the Serbians did in the 1990s under Milosevic, some of that was revenge against the Croatians for the horrors of World War Two. And of course, as always, religion played a hand in the dirty dealing, as it always does when stupid people go to war, believing that Jesus speaks through Hitler or Milosevic or Stalin or name a hundred other demagogues, empty worthless windbags who leave only death and destruction." She stopped to catch her breath. "They are all gone now—Anna Maria, Chetko, Stana, even your little tiny sister—so I can speak freely because this village is cleaner without him. They're all gone."

"So what was so terrible about that family?" Hannah asked, holding her father's journal under her palms.

"It wasn't the family. They were no better or worse than any of us. It was Chetko who brought evil with him." Frau Jones leaned close to continue her story in a low voice; even in a small village there were secrets. "We were all in bad shape after the war. Those were desperate times. Then along came this foreigner, this Croatian, Chetko, who was on the run from police in several countries. He always reeked of beer and had his chin and nose in the air, a real bully, poking at you, while he pronounced stupid things—a demagogue with power only over his wife and children—but he was fiendishly clever. He told a lot of lies about himself, and managed to go to work for the Americans. A lot of people here worked for the U.S. as Local National civilians. Many of them stole tools, furniture, anything they could from the Americans. Like a cargo cult; they felt it was owed to them, without any reason. Chetko and some of his cronies had a red-hot black market bazaar going in the area."

"Always a criminal," Rob said.

Frau Jones nodded. "If only he had shot himself when it was over for the Nazis in Croatia, like Hitler did in Berlin." She paused to sip her coffee. "Anna Maria was a simple, empty-headed young girl. She married Chetko, and lived all her life here in the village until she died not long ago. She never drove a car, and the farthest she ever traveled was Heidelberg. She was a true villager, a peasant. They had two daughters, one of them Stanislava, the other a girl named Karin who ran away as a teenager and never came back. She died far away years later Now comes the most terrible part of this story, apart from the death of your baby sister Klara.

"When Stana was about twelve years old, back in the early 1960s, her parents had been married for years, and Chetko treated his wife like dirt. She was a simple village girl and put up with it—on the surface for others to see. But Anna Maria, who was pretty, began running around with other men behind Chetko's back." She paused to let that sink in. "Imagine how an egomaniac like Chetko would take that."

After a pause, she continued, in a frail, reluctant, but determined voice. "The two innocent young girls Stana and Karin were asleep in an upstairs bedroom near their parent's bedroom. Their mother was out running around with a well-off married U.S. Army colonel from Heidelberg, who took her to fancy restaurants and screwed her in hotels down there. So Chetko, who was out a tavern with his ex-SS cronies near the main railroad station—drunk as a fish as usual, and coldly handling it well—heard about his wife's activities. And with one of the Americans yet, whom he hated so much! In a rage, he drove back here to the village, went into the bedroom, and raped both girls." She nodded. "Out of hate and rage and revenge, this drunken monster raped both of his children, in an effort to hurt his wife. It's a wonder he didn't kill the two girls."

"Oh my god," Hannah said. "They were how old?"

"Stana was thirteen, I think, and Karin was twelve."

Rob added: "No wonder he hated Dan Wilson—a U.S. soldier."

A pause descended as those around the table sought to digest this information. Hannah could begin to understand the inferno from hell that her father had walked into. He was a soldier assigned to Heidelberg, and couldn't simply leave. He was working for a staff of men who were oblivious at best, hard-hearted and cruel at worst. *Poor Daniel Wilson.*

"Now you know why Karin ran away and never came back. Stana however became alcoholic like her father. It's what they call Stockholm Syndrome. The victim identifies with the evil-doer. The whole family went into psychiatric counseling paid for by our national health insurance. For years, they were under the care of a doctor down in Heidelberg, which after all has one of the finest universities and medical centers in the world. Anna Maria and Chetko stayed together. He never physically harmed his daughters again, but he bullied his family and everyone else with his usual words and swaggering and sharp tongue and bitter sayings."

Rob looked sick. "Why did they all put up with him?"

"We was very clever, very quick, and could turn your own words around on you. He always had words to stick into someone, like a knife, goading a person—which is what he did of course to your father as well. He rarely came in here. Nobody in the village wanted anything to do with him, even though they didn't know the secret of his family's horrible rape and incest." She paused. "So Stana did not handle it well, and became an alcoholic. She hated herself, I think, as much as she claimed to love her father, who destroyed her life. She only went out with destructive, drunken, brutal young men. One of

Stana's young boyfriends, also a U.S. soldier or airman, I forget which, actually was so drunk that when Chetko kept goading him as they sat in living room, with that viper tongue of his, digging in to cut the boy at his weaknesses—Chetko was so skilled at finding out where those weak spots in the soul were, and he could cut you like a surgeon to get at your pain—that young man slit his wrists a few hours later and almost bled to death in their living room. Still, Stana never learned anything. Karin had long since run away. Anna Maria and her daughter Stana stayed with the ship as it was going down."

"And then my Dad came along," Hannah said.

"Yes. It is a mystery to me. I have tried to read his journal that I have given to you, but none of it makes sense. It is almost like there is a missing journal." She pointed. "He called that one Journal II."

"And we have Journal III," Hannah said. "That's the story of his happy marriage after returning to the U.S. He found happiness with Nancy."

"Your dear mother," Frau Jones gushed. "And you two beautiful children. I am so happy for Dan."

"There must have been a Journal I before this," Rob said.

"We know he was a broken man when he came home," Hannah said. "Now I am starting to finally get a sense of what he got himself involved with. What a shame, in a region so beautiful as our Neckar Valley, to be so miserable as he must have been."

"Your Dad was devoted," Frau Jones said. "He was young, and immature, and he had a strong sense of duty. In his journal, he writes about how he felt the obligation to stay with Stana because he made her pregnant. They were married very quickly after they met. It's a difficult story, too. Apparently, Dan had another woman in Paris. I know nothing about that. There is one reference in Journal II, but it's as if he tore some pages out to hide all that. Who knows why. Oh." She snapped her fingers. "It was a French woman named Claudette. She was his age, and Stana's age, though Stana and this French girl never met as far as I know.

"The French girl was studying here in Heidelberg at the university. Very brilliant young woman, like your Dad, far too intelligent for the likes of Stana and her parents. Karin, the sister who escaped, was smarter, but your Dad never met Karin, and nobody here ever saw her again. I heard Karin died in South America a few years ago, so Karin is out of the picture. Dan Wilson was in love with both Stana and Claudette. He was torn between the two. The French girl returned to Paris and continued her studies at the Louvre or someplace. That is all I know.

"Your father married Stana, who was pregnant by him, and Danny wanted to stay, take responsibility, and do the right thing no matter what. Stana's parents hated Americans, the way real village idiots and bullies hate anyone who is different, especially if they think the person is somehow smarter or better because they themselves are cow shit, which they only admit to themselves deep down. Chetko could not stop saying horrible things about Americans, including a lot of lies about the Jews and all the usual Nazi hallucinations that village idiots love to hear.

"Always with that tone, mocking, cutting, chin up in the air as if challenging you, cutting you, bullying you, goading—and those icy cold pig eyes. I shudder to think what atrocities that snake joined in Croatia before he slithered away to our poor village. Anna Maria, the cow, went along with anything Chetko said, so she and Chetko worked on Stana not to stay with Danny. Even though Danny was the only good guy who ever came along for the poor girl, though she was usually too drunk and hurting to know that.

"Poor Stana didn't want the baby and tried to abort it herself. Abortion was illegal in West Germany, and she couldn't afford to travel to Poland, which is Catholic but was run by Communists. In the end, who knows if her drinking did it, or if she got hold of some drugs, or what, but the baby was born with a heart defect.

"Suddenly they all became saints. Anna Maria became a dedicated grandmother, poor delusional drunken Stana became a model mother. Every day they went to the medical center, where Klara lived half her short life in a infant intensive care unit. Drunken Stana blamed Danny, and yet Danny stayed devoted to his wife and daughter. Danny could not simply pick up and leave. He was stuck here in the Army, and they treated him very badly also. He was working for some snake of a lieutenant who was an insecure, malignant sociopath—"

"Chetko's evil U.S. twin," Rob guessed, as he remembered reading bitter hints in the Journal.

"Something like that; and a senior sergeant from the South who hated northerners and spoke under his breath of the South seceding again. So he also hated Danny for those reasons, and spoke gloatingly to Danny's face about how he would be bankrupt for the rest of his life because of his sick baby."

Rob said: "How could he get away with that?"

Frau Jones said: "You know they talk in code, from both sides of their heads, your Southerners, and False Jesus is on their side no matter how many Negroes they drag to death behind their trucks, castrate, burn alive, or torture for hours while their wives and children watch proudly and take photographs and recite Bible verses. You have many Chetkos among you, some in the top levels of government these days. You see why my husband and I had no regrets moving back to Heidelberg."

"You don't like the South," Rob said with equanimity.

"Does it show? Detroit was bad enough. Your South is one big Croatia, and their Ustasha simply wear white sheets. All so pious and full of hate and ignorance. *Mir gruselts*. I get gruesome shivers just thinking about it all. This is still my home, what I am used to."

Hannah sighed. "I saw those ruins in Heidelberg and couldn't imagine why people would stoop to so much death and destruction."

Rob said: "Snapshot—the whole history of the human race, and even here in this village. I think the majority of people would live in peace and prosperity, but the Hitlers and the Stupid People always destroy the world around them; while the money people behind the scenes build weapons, loan money, and march around in field marshal uniforms."

"If only people would learn from our mistakes," Frau Jones said. "You Americans wrote our Constitution for us, and it is more democratic than what you have. We are smarter than we were a century ago. But look, about your Dad.

"After little baby Klara died, Danny wouldn't let anyone from his office attend his daughter's funeral. He said it would kill him to have that filthy lieutenant and that dirty sergeant show up at his child's funeral in all of their hypocrisy and snake-like falseness. Probably to stand among mourners and gloat over their victim's further misfortune.

"He told me all this, at a table in this restaurant, in tears half the time. He would have gladly left, but he would have been arrested as a deserter. His life would have been ruined with a dishonorable discharge.

"And he was so far from home, so lonely, he had nobody to talk to. He would go for long walks by himself in the forests around here, on Sundays when he was free, just to get away from everything and run away from his own thoughts.

"The baby, named Klara, or Claire, did not live a full year. She died in the medical center here in Heidelberg. You have no real health care in your country. A crime against logic and humanity—incomprehensible that you put up with it. The Army would not provide for her in their hospitals after Danny's return to civilian life. Danny's own Army doctor, very sympathetic, told him that the Army would ship her back to the United States and ultimately put her in some civilian place that would charge a fortune. That snake from the South knew this, and gloated; told Danny he would be bankrupt for life back in the USA. Danny made a tough decision to let her stay in the German system, which made his hateful in-laws happy. The German medical system did everything humanly possible, including flying in the country's top surgeon from Berlin to operate. Danny told me they implanted a heart valve from somewhere in the United States. Some child in that same city in California could not receive that heart valve because her family could not afford it in your barbaric system. After the operation here in

Heidelberg, Klara lived a few more days but slipped away during the night. Her tiny body could not handle the stress."

"Her grave is gone," Rob said.

The old woman nodded. "After your father left, it was Chetko's last revenge. At twenty-eight years, if you don't renew the payment, they throw away the gravestones. They let the grave go to seed, and eventually bury someone else in it. Anna Maria might have wanted to pay to keep her granddaughter's pretty marble stone with Klara's name on it in brushed steel letters, but Chetko would hold forth with his chin in the air, pushing and goading, stabbing with that knife of a thick yellow finger, saying it was best to kill of the last memories of the American who had invaded their home, or words like that. I don't know if Danny ever came back here, but after twenty-eight years he would be shocked to find they had thrown Klara's gravestone away as if she never really mattered."

"What happened to the stone?" Rob asked.

"It went to the stone breaker down by the river, who crushed it into rubble to cover driveways or build taverns. Nobody knows or cares."

Hannah sat mutely, horrified.

Frau Jones added: "Chetko gave your father's memory, and his granddaughter's, one more kick in the ribs."

They all sat silently contemplating these gloomy details.

"There is one more thing."

After a minute's silence, Frau Jones continued: "Danny told me that as the baby died, about one in the morning, he was here in the village in his and Stana's little *Stube*, staying up late by the wood stove, and writing in his journal. He and Stana had an apartment near Chetko and Anna Maria, because by then, Stana had already given up on her marriage and simply wanted to be drunk and stay near her parents. It wasn't that she hated Danny so much, as she hated herself. And that was done to her by Chetko, the monster and war criminal, who died here a few years ago never having a shred of repentance. Absolutely no remorse, no connection to other human beings. Brain wired differently. Defective, like a robot, but evil and conniving amid all his bluster and shallowness." She paused a moment. "Many of us may live in villages, but we do have the Internet and news services. We listen well, those of us who do listen.

"So back to that evening. Danny had been drinking. Stana was passed out in the bedroom of the apartment, drunk. At about one a.m., Danny felt a terrible urgency and rose. He felt it was time to get down to Heidelberg to the medical center. He knew that Klara, the little infant, was dying at that moment. You have to understand. I talked with both Danny and with Stana at various times. Klara would have been a beautiful, brilliant woman. Already as a baby she could look you in the eyes and laugh if you laughed, or look at you seriously if you were telling her something important. She had charisma."

Frau Jones' eyes were rimmed, red, with sadness and joy as she told this story.

"I know there was one happy moment in all that sadness, when Stana and Danny sat with Klara on Stana's lap at the hospital. The baby spent half her brief life in the hospital. Klara was having such a wonderful little day. She kept laughing gurgling as Stana bounced her gently on her lap, and the three of them laughed, and laughed, and laughed together as one joyous soul. As they three laughed, the two young parents were simultaneously bathed in tears of tragedy because they knew in their souls that this was the only such moment their little baby would ever have.

"It lasted ten minutes, from what both Stana and Danny told me, but it was the happiest moment in Klara's short life, and maybe the only happy moment in that sad marriage. And thank God for the wonderful young German nurses who took care of all those infants. Some of them were orphans, abandoned, most of them born with conditions they were dying from. Same old story—parents lost souls as well—alcoholics, on drugs, or dead. Those nurses gave these little babies the only love they ever knew.

"So after the baby died, Stana turned completely away from Danny. He was stuck in the army, working for some miserable people who had no shred of sympathy or understanding. The saying was: if the army wanted you to have a baby, they would have issued you one. Same thing about marriage. Danny buried himself in work until he could reach his departure…"

"His ETS," Rob said in a flash of understanding.

"His Estimated Time of Separation," Hannah said. *Aha!*

"Yes, and when he left, Stana barely said goodbye. Like her mother many years earlier, she was already flirting and running around with other American soldiers, including one whose marriage she ruined after Danny was gone from the picture; but she had been flirting with that next guy in Danny's presence before his ETS. Stana and her trashy family were all relieved to see Danny go, for reasons that can only be explained by the fact that they were ignorant peasants, and Danny was different, so they didn't understand him. He was studying for his Master's with a major U.S. university's overseas division, and they accused him of laziness because he studied for hours rather than doing village work like cutting and stacking wood or cleaning the yard. He brought an air of change, and they hated it. All Americans are on drugs and no good, they told him openly, Chetko with that chin in the air, prodding and bullying to cause insult and hurt. So Danny left, and…"

"Yes?"

"I never saw him again. I worried about him all these years. I am so happy to hear that he had a beautiful life after his horror here."

"He never got over it," Rob said. "I understand it now, finally."

"Me too," Hannah said.

"Stana did run around with a few other men, but nothing lasting. She kept drinking, stayed at home, and died as an older village spinster with a cigarette in one hand and a glass of raw vodka in the other. Maybe she got drugs also down in Heidelberg running around with stray G.I.s. Who knows. They are all dead and gone now. All of them."

Almost all, Hannah thought, thinking of the mature woman whose voice had sounded in Danny's head as his baby daughter died. *Her ghost. An angel from another world, where she lived, and grew up into a strong woman of great accomplishments.*

"Now we know," Rob and Hannah said in one voice, being twins.

Frau Jones added: "There are still mysteries. Like who was the woman in Paris? I think her name was Claudette something. And… what I often remember as I already said. Danny told me that, at the moment when his baby girl was dying, he felt a terrible urgency to run across the street to get his parents-in-law and drive to the hospital. But then a wonderful and strange thing happened."

"What?"

"A woman spoke in his head. He knew in his heart, without any doubt, that it was Klara, or Claire, but it was the voice and persona of a grownup woman with a life of her own, a good life from the sound of her, a solid and decent woman with a wonderful personality like the baby had. It was her adult self, that she would have become, and she said to Danny in his head: *It's all right. Don't go. Everything will happen as it must, and there is nothing we can do. Farewell, until we meet again. There are other chapters yet to be written in this book.* Or words like that. Danny told me all about it. They weren't words exactly, but thoughts, and they came from her mind to his mind by some form of ESP or ghost language. Angel talk. Angel means messenger in Greek, you know…"

At that, Frau Jones tapered off. She looked worn out, overcome, and shaken. Irma and another woman helped her rise. She said her goodbyes, whispering that she was overjoyed to see Danny's two beautiful twin children, and hoped that Danny and Nancy were happy together in heaven looking down on Rob and Hannah.

⁞ ● ◌

After Frau Jones had been helped to her home, Frau Hagel told Rob and Hannah not to worry—the bill was on the house. She even offered to pack ham and cheese rolls for them, along with cold coffee in a thermal bottle that Jack would bring back whenever it suited him. "And do not forget your father's journal, which he forgot here so many decades ago."

They thanked her, but declined her generosity, and after hugs and kisses as if they'd known each other for years, they headed back down the mountain to *Ödendorf*. Hannah clutched Dad's Journal II to her chest with both arms.

Along the gloomy road, thick, dark trees rustled their crowns all around them in a disturbed, nervous wind that seemed full of messages and portents. More of those autumn leaves roiled around on the road as the van drove downhill. Something more was yet to come, Hannah thought. What had Frau Jones said—a woman in Paris named Claudette. But what did it mean? And how did one scratch at the surface of that deep mystery?

At his village, they thanked Jack profusely. He admitted this had been one of the most profound days for him in recent years. From there, Rob drove his car back down to Heidelberg. They hung out together for an hour or so, but had no real desire to be tourists or play. So Rob drove back to Frankfurt, and Hannah took her train back to Paris with the precious Journal II in her suitcase.

9.　　Fulgent Moon in Paris

Hannah called Yves the moment she returned to Paris. This time she was even more deeply disturbed than after returning from Dad's funeral. More than ever, she wanted to leave that hideous history behind her, and hide in her normal little daily life in the City of Lights.

Her wonderful boyfriend was there for her in every way. He seemed to sense her pain, and responded by being loving and philosophical and supportive. He vowed to stay close to her as much as possible. He asked if she wanted him to come over, and she said yes if he didn't mind that she was so exhausted in body and soul from her emotional journey to Heidelberg and her father's past.

While waiting for Yves to hurry over, Hannah spoke with Rob over the phone. Rob called to tell her he'd arrived safely. He was just then at the apartment of his beautiful, sensitive, serious-eyed Elise from Luxembourg who was also totally supportive.

Before midnight, Hannah lay in bed, sleeping exhaustedly with Yves spooning behind her like a comforting wall of safety and warmth..

But they were not alone.

ജ ● ൽ

The window to Hannah's small apartment was open just a trifle, and a breeze blew the curtain. In the blue-black, clear air a nearly full moon glowed with brilliant, fulgent light so pure it almost seemed to go past warm yellow into icy white.

The growing moon had something special about it that radiated warmth like the sun, whose light it mirrored; something even more than Parisian poets and composers had felt as they were inspired by that clarity of *la Lune*.

As the curtains fluttered silently, a feminine form took shape in the room. Seated at the desk near the window was that same angel, a woman with golden-dark hair. The angel's name was Claire, like in Claude Debussy's 1890 *Claire de Lune*, from his *Suite des Bergamasques*, meaning reveries and dances of clowns, in an age of modernism conflicted with industrial destruction, when artists in Paris began to turn away from realism toward surrealism, absurdism, and other fantastic modes. The title Clear or Bright

Moon, or simply Moonlight, was based on a famous 1869 poem by Paul Verlaine that inspired the likes of Rimbaud, Ravel, Fauré, and many other creative souls of that now-lost age. Paul Verlaine's famous poem in translation could be rendered thus:

Clair de Lune
(Moonlight)

Your tender soul is a twilight landscape
where masques and bergamasques dance,
plucking strings; looking oh so slightly
    sad in happy costumes,

as they sing in some minor clef
about finding love and happiness.

Their song weaves melancholy
    with moonlight...

    ...quiet moonlight so sad and so lovely
that it makes birds dream in their trees,
while fountains sob in ecstasy
    'mid slender pillars and marble statues.

-- Paul Verlaine
Paris, 1869
Translated by Jean-Thomas Cullen 2017

Claire (Klara in another time, another world) was willowy, of medium to tall height, with slender arms and legs. She wore a pale dress of no particular color in that sharply cut, almost glassy moonlight. The back, as she sat bending over the desk, was cut low and revealed a row of strong but delicate vertebrae under smooth young skin. She rested her elbows on the desk and appeared to be thinking.

Her elegant, narrow face looked perplexed. Golden-blonde hair hung in curving bass clefs (keys) over each cheek, pointing to the corners of her lightly lipsticked mouth. Her hair bounced in curly treble-clefs in the shadows of the room, and in the lunar halo around her finely shaped head.

A moment later, her deeply serious, masterful eyes widened in a lunar glow of inspiration. She became Athena, virgin goddess who fights at the forefront among the fiercest warriors, yet bakes a nice cake and is the most wise among lawgivers. She was Klara or Claire, Moon Goddess, breathing the vapors of Diana and Artemis, but for a moment the helmeted goddess of iron beauty stepped into her, for whom the city of Athens is named, and whose Parthenon (Temple of the Virgin) sits atop the crowning hill.

Klara reached for the Journal her father had written in Heidelberg, which her sister had brought to Paris. Opening it to the first few pages, she idly rifled with long, pretty fingers through Hannah's cup of pens and pencils. Avoiding the pens, which might smear, she chose a hard No. 1 pencil and with that she wrote a few cryptic words in the margin. She half wrote, half-printed in a hand much resembling Daniel Wilson's. She wrote: *Claudette Vervain, 45 Rue de la Belle Ferronière, Paris 75012.*

With that, the Classical goddesses vanished, back to their statues all around Paris.

Once again just Klara—Clarity—she rose without a sound. She let the pencil drop, letting it silently drop onto the open page and roll away, falling off the back of the desk and disappearing forever in darkness along the wall to create yet another tiny mystery.

Claire rose and drifted like the wind-blown curtains—a fleeting figure that seemed to float, though her limbs moved as if she were walking gracefully on bare feet, perhaps in another world. She walked a few steps and vanished into the wall, lighter than a cherub's giggle.

Hannah sighed in her sleep, as if the breeze coming from the window had gently disturbed her, as it moved the curtains with a light touch. Hannah remained curled up in Yves' embrace. The two sleepers were bathed in moonlight as they slept soundly, with faint smiles on their bright features, and dreamt of masques and bergamasques.

⃣ ● ⃤

In the morning, Hannah called in sick at work and took a long soak in the tub. She threw on her standard little Parisian summer dress with white heels and a headkerchief, dabbed on light makeup, and took the elevator downstairs. She walked briskly along the sidewalk on her block near Passy, and sat at a table outside her favorite corner restaurant. She ordered a quick breakfast of croissants, butter, jam, ham, and cheese along with strong coffee. Rejuvenated by a crisp morning breeze, she took a walk around the block. Then she went back upstairs to her flat and circled around, doing little of anything, until she focused on the journal lying open on her desk.

Despite all the painful explanations and confessions in Verlorenau, something was missing and incomplete here. What had Daddy said so often as he appeared to want more of life than life was willing to give?

There are more chapters yet to be written in this story…

She read through the sparse, disjointed notes and entries. Nothing was really chronological, at least not specifically by day and date. Sometimes, Dad had scribbled a date in the margin. It was a journal of pain and darkness, composed in Zum Forst near the end of his time in the Army and Germany.

The journal began with the words: "At the Bridge of Regret in Paris, I made the worst decision of my life. I can't allow myself to regret the joy of having Klara with us, a bright gurgling happy baby even as she was turning blue from lack of oxygen due to the heart condition. Klara made the most of her short life. She was a hero. I somehow have to write down all for her sake and if I have children again, if I get married after my ETS. Leaving here, back to the World, will be a relief beyond description. I will be reborn, walking the streets of Portland where I grew up…"

Children… that's me and Rob. Hannah rose, slammed the journal shut, and strode around the room. It was painful to absorb even a paragraph of it that he had written amid tears in the dark forest above Heidelberg. She resolved to digest every word of it.

She called Rob. "I started reading it. I can't read more than a page or so without wanting to cry."

He said distantly in Frankfurt: "Can you make a copy and FAX it to me? I'm curious."

"Sure. Two heads are better than one." She added: "I keep getting the feeling there was something before, like he broke off suddenly. He mentions a Bridge of Regret here in Paris. We know he had a woman here also, whom he abandoned to marry Stana because of the baby, I suppose."

Rob said: "We have a Journal III and a Journal II. There has to be a Journal I. But where?"

She shook her head. "I'm going for a long walk. We'll talk more later."

୨୦ • ଓଷ

In the evenings, when she was alone, or when Yves lay on her bed reading, she'd take a magnifying glass and started again poring over the Journal II that Frau Jones had given her in greater Heidelberg.

"Go easy," Yves counseled from the bed.

She sighed. "I know. I have to stop reading when my eyes get blurry with tears."

"Why don't you come over here and snuggle with me?"

"Wait." She sat up suddenly, training the magnifying glass on a faint bit of writing on one side in the early pages. "I can barely make this out. It's written in very light pencil. What does it say?" She bit the tip of her tongue and hovered in close, bringing the magnifying glass up and down. "I have it. It's a name." She looked more closely yet. "A name and an address."

Yves rose and padded over on stocking feet. He put one arm around her shoulder, nuzzling cheek to cheek (and she raised an arm to embrace him in welcome of his comfort, while handing him the glass).

He read: *Claudette Vervain, 45 Rue de la Ferronière, Paris 75012.*

She snapped her fingers, remembering Frau Jones' words. "Claudette. I think that was the name of his Parisian girlfriend, who studied in Heidelberg for a year long ago."

Yves shook his head. He laid the magnifier down. "If she was his age, she'd be in her seventies."

"She might still be around. Look, we have an address."

"Sounds familiar somehow. I'll look it up on the Internet."

She pulled her laptop close, and rose to give him her seat. Yves opened up the shell, powered up, and plugged away on the keyboard. He began commenting as he found out details: "It's a small street in the Twelfth Arrondissement. I've never heard of that street, but there are thousands in the city and I only know some of the ones in my neighborhood."

They researched until they found the address. It was not far from the newly reinvigorated area of Bercy, a former quarter of wine warehouses and the like, which had been turned into an attraction called Bercy Village for both tourists and locals.

80 • CR

Next time Yves had the car out, they took a drive east into the Twelfth Arrondissement for a lark. The street, near the Rue de l'Alouette and the Bois de Vincennes, was an alley inside a stone tunnel leading to a courtyard It was one of those tucked-away corners that one finds at odd places in Paris, always a surprise to stumble upon when one does. The number was old and rusty, white lettering on a small blue enameled square, on a mossy stuccoed wall near the tunnel's end, beside a beat-up looking old steel door with rivets and metal straps for security.

Meanwhile, Hannah also did a search on the name Vervain. She came up with various persons of that name, along with references to the beautiful flower verbena, but no Claudette Vervain, and nowhere near that address. Further searches in the broader Île-de-France and then in other French cities yielded no meaningful results. Nothing jumped out.

Puzzled, Hannah pushed the journal aside and went on with her life, which was busy enough.

80 • CR

How happy Dad and Mom would be to see their kids now, Hannah thought as she and Yves strolled arm in arm along the Seine near the Notre Dame de Paris cathedral. The bells rang and thundered musically as if in a salute. She was once again happy to be back in her own life, as he had been after the funeral in Oregon only weeks earlier.

Paris felt like home now. She loved the city, with all of its beautiful and gritty aspects. It could be a sunny city at times, and then a gray one. Often a playful one, like when the authorities brought in sand and created an artificial beach on the wharves of the Seine.

It was great to be back to work, to be in harness and back to normal. She relished her rides in the Métro and RER train networks. She loved her walks at lunch under the great square arch newly built to complement the classical

Axis running from the Tuileries Park through the Arc de Triomphe and across the river to la Défense.

80 • CR

On their day off, she and Yves took a twenty-minute stroll past the Île de Paris with its Notre Dame cathedral and the Sainte-Chapelle. They strolled on the Quai Anatole France along the Left Bank.

Hannah never suspected that this would be yet another day that changed her life forever.

They crossed the Seine at the Pont de la Concorde, and arrived on the Right Bank at the Place de la Concorde. This had been a cobblestone place of horror from 1789 forward, when thousands of royalists, notables, and aristocrats including King Louis XVI and his wife, Queen Marie-Antoinette, were beheaded in a steady sequence before howling mobs as the cobblestones flowed with blood. The square was initially renamed *Place de la Revolution* and soon afterward, in 1795, received the title of reconciliation that would stick with it for centuries: *Place de la Concorde*, or Square of Harmony.

From that square, which retained almost nothing of its violent history, Hannah and Yves strolled into the broad tree-lined lanes of the Tuileries Gardens with their fountains and ponds and many famous statues. Passing the Arc du Carrousel (a smaller version of the Arc de Triomphe) they entered the main square of the Louvre with its modern, glassy pyramid. They stopped at the Café Richelieu for espresso and a little light pastry. From there—picking up a free tour brochure as a reference, because as Yves said, you could live here all your life and never see everything in the Louvre—they let the whims of the day, and fate, carry them wherever the winds might take them.

80 • CR

According to a brochure available at the entry, the Tuileries Gardens are all that is left in modern times of a 16th Century palace built by Catherine de Medici, widow of King Henri II (who died in 1559 in a tournament at an older palace to the east, as allegedly predicted by Nostradamus at the time). The name Tuileries was a reference to a row of tile-baking kilns (*tuileries*).

The Tuileries Palace was burned to the ground by during the Paris Commune anarchy after France lost the Franco-Prussian War in 1871, causing the fall of Napoleon Bonaparte's vainglorious imperial nephew Emperor Napoleon III, and a bloody civil war before the Third Republic was formalized in the Constitution of 1875. Today, as Hannah and Yves walked through the beautiful grounds, only the Tuileries Gardens remained on their way into the Louvre. Like so much of Paris, it was a matter of beauty being built upon horror, spring after winter, life upon death. And life goes on, as the saying tells us.

ഇ • ഇ

As Hannah and Yves strolled thorough the grand galleries of the Louvre, on the first level in the Denon Wing, they made the obligatory pilgrimage past the world's most famous painting. Some instinct told them this was a key target on their trajectory in the mystery set in motion years ago while their father was still young, and the last time he saw the love of his life, Claudette, was on the Bridge of Regret right in front of the Louvre.

It was not only a day off, but a touristy day, so they had to thread their way among thousands of milling people including tour groups from around the world. Tour leaders held up signs on selfie-sticks, and the signs typically had a tiny national flag and the country of the tour group. These included Japanese, Chinese, Egyptians, Canadians, U.S. groups, and more. Yves flaunted a *presse* or *media* pass because of his video work, and they got in ahead of the crowd.

"I'm always so thrilled to go in here," Hannah said as she held Yves by the elbow and they strode in, holding each other close. "I love walking through the gardens first."

"Me too," Yves said. Nearby, tour boats glided past on the Seine, slipping under the Pont des Arts—one the world's most famous passerelles, or pedestrian foot bridges.

"It's the world's largest and most visited art museum," Yves said proudly while holding her close. "Tens of thousands of artifacts from the Old Stone Age to the present.

There she was, the *Mona Lisa*, smiling coyly behind protective plate glass and flanked by at least one armed guard and a museum curator at all times. Hannah and Yves sat on a bench nearby, letting the hordes of tourists wander past in groups. Oddly, somehow, as if a ghostly hand had placed it there, another brochure sort of brushed up against Hannah (as if wind-blown, although there was no breeze inside the museum). She picked it up, and there it was in brief: a quick recounting of the story of Leonardo da Vinci's masterpiece.

Leonardo da Vinci (1452-1419) was a strange man, and a talented genius. As the brochure related, his life is as much shrouded in mystery on some accounts, as it shines across the ages for his accomplishments. He was not only a gifted artist, but a scientific one. He was one of the first to dissect corpses (as legally as that could be accomplished in late Renaissance and Early Modern Italy or France) so that he could study the technology and biology of muscles and nerves—all the better to realistically paint them. He wanted to understand their facial and other musculature from the ground up, on a technical and mechanical level.

He made studies of heads to get the expressions right. He drew engines of war and technological innovations of many kinds, including submarines and tanks and the like. Historians regard him as the true exemplar of a Universal Genius or Renaissance Man, who was interested in many subjects, dabbled in many disciplines, and made brilliant contributions in everything he touched.

Leonardo was born out of wedlock to very ordinary parents: a local notary (Piero Da Vinci, or Peter of Vinci, whose very place name—from the Latin *vicus*, neighborhood—connotes a sort of nook or corner tucked away out of sight near Florence). His mother was a peasant named Caterina. The young boy showed so much talent that he gained apprenticeship in the school of the famous painter Andrea del Verrocchio, whose name 'True Eye' was a nickname, like so many in an age when people didn't have last names. For much the same reason, Leonardo became stuck with the monicker 'from Vinci' which might as well have been something like 'from Podunk.' He overcame his humble beginnings, and is remembered as one of history's great geniuses.

Leonardo lived for sixty-seven years, a respectable figure for a man of his age in which so many did not make it half so long. The last few years of that time, he lived in France not too far from Paris. There, he completed his most important final painting under puzzling circumstances, without pay. That became the world's most famous painting: *La Gioconda*, or Smiling One (a pun on the patron's name del Giocondo), the so-called *Mona Lisa*, which had been the property of the Kings of France for centuries, later of the French people, and here it was, hanging in its own special room in the Louvre.

       ଗ • ଓଃ

The brochure could only touch on the highlights of Leonardo's life. What Hannah was most curious about, as she sat next to Yves on the upholstered bench, was how a Renaissance Italian master's paintings—for example, the *Mona Lisa* and *La Belle Ferronnière* among others—could have wound up hanging in the Louvre in Paris.

Then she remembered the brochure that had been dropped by her side on the bench in the Square Viviani. That brochure told the outlines of the story. Da Vinci, a Florentine Italian, who worked in Florence and Milan during his early life, was more or less adopted by the King of France. Leonardo turned 48 years old in 1500, reaching the height of his artistic and intellectual powers. By then, he had his own small group of close assistants, most notably the young artist-journeymen Salai and Francesco Melzi who became the executors and heirs to some of his works. Part of the aura of mystique about Leonardo is that he never married, nor are there any significant love relationships attributed to him, aside from some hints of gay scandal that got him arrested once in his early twenties with several young noblemen, a case soon quashed by one boy's wealthy family.

From 1513 to 1516, Leonardo (aged 61 to 64) brought his *atelier* south to Rome, where he worked closely with Michelangelo and Raphael under the sponsorship of Pope Leo X. Leonardo had several things in common with the pope, including their origins in Florence. While Leonardo was from the lower end of society, this particular pope was a prominent member of the Medici family—the same family from which Catherine de Medici, wife of the late Henri II of France, had come.

In the early 1500s, powerful King François I of France (father of Henri II killed half a century later in the jousting tournament) was successfully campaigning against the disunited city states in northern Italy. The pope met with him in Bologna, presumably to negotiate for the preservation of the Papal States in central Italy, as well as a favorable peace in relation to his aristocratic and republican enemies as a Medici. Through the Pope, Leonardo became acquainted with King François, who commissioned Leonardo in 1515 to build him a sort of robotic metal lion. Within a year (1516), Leonardo had moved to France where he became a permanent fixture at the Château d'Amboise, in the Loire Valley not far south of Paris and its surrounding Île-de-France. The Loire Valley, which runs roughly east-west for 170 miles (280 km) is famous for its picturesque countryside and romantic cities. It is a land of vinyards, fruit trees, and all manner of vegetables and farm produce. It includes a belt of storied ancient and medieval cities like Amboise, Angers, Blois, Chinon, Orléans, Saumur, and Tours. In many of his estates, the powerful new King François installed famous painters and artisans—none more famous than Leonardo.

80 • 03

Leonardo lived near the fabulous castle of Amboise for the last three years of his life. More precisely, he was given a smaller, ancillary mansion called the Château du Clos Lucé, connected to the royal chateau by an underground passageway. Today, Leonardo's home away from home was a museum of his works.

He died in bed presumably from cardiovascular problems on May 2, 1519. According to legend, King François was at his bedside, and cradled a dying Leonardo's head.

After Leonardo's death, his main possessions were split up (not without the usual rancor) between his assistants Melzi and Salai, and his brothers back in Florence. There is some controversy about the exact path taken by Leonardo's several famous paintings at Amboise, most notably the *Mona Lisa*. The Louvre, in any case, claims that it became property of King François in 1518.

And now, reading the brochure, Hannah noticed a tiny footnote at the bottom of the last page. Her gaze was directed there by a little asterisk in the text above, relating to the various controversies about how and why Leonardo painted her.

Startled, Hannah read the footnote. The text seemed obscure and did not particularly grab her attention. What did get her notice were several scholarly references in incredibly tiny italic print at the end of the footnote. These included a graduate assistant Claudette Vervain, Department of Late Renaissance and Early Modern Paintings, at the Louvre.

"*Oh, my, aching, lord,*" Hannah enunciated in hammer-blow wording.

"What's the matter now?" Yves asked with a pained look.

"I found her."

"The *Mona Lisa*?"

"No, Claudette Vervain. Dad's girlfriend in Paris, the love of his life."

Yves managed a stunned look. "I have something else to show you."

"What is it?" she asked, almost impatiently. What could merit her attention at a moment like this?

He pointed to another brochure, this one being of Leonardo's works in the Louvre. He pointed to a painting of a provocative, characterful young woman. The painting's title was *Portrait of an Unknown Woman*, or *La Belle Ferronnière*. She was not La Gioconda, but she did have that mysterious little smile filled with secret thoughts that marked Leonard's craft at its highest, informed by his careful studies of living people as well as his scientific dissection of cadavers to research how muscles worked, including those of smiling and frowning.

Something tickled at Hannah's memory. "What am I thinking?"

"The address written in your Dad's Journal II along with Claudette Vervain's name."

A light flickered on in Hannah's mind. "Rue de la Belle Ferronière." She remembered that pretty little headband on the unknown mistress' forehead with the jewel in the center. At the same time, Hannah recalled a mental snapshot of the hidden street near Bercy, with its wall in the tunnel leading into the courtyard; that steel door; and its secretive atmosphere.

"Probably just a strange coincidence," Yves ventured.

"Maybe," she allowed softly. "Or is it?"

"You're scaring me."

"Listen, Yves, it's almost as if someone has been guiding me toward whatever is coming next. We're here, and we found a reference to Claudette Vervain. My father wrote her address in his journal, and the address is a street with the same name as one of Leonardo's famous paintings here in the Louvre."

"La Belle Ferronnière?" Yves leaved through the brochures until he found one describing Leonardo's other (but far less) famous paintings in the Louvre, including the one of the Lovely Ferronnière. He showed her the text.

"It's not the woman, but that little headband with a tiny jewel in the center of her forehead. Look at that seductive, scheming face. Her personality comes across after five centuries. She was young, and a mistress of King François I. She was a commoner, whose husband was supposedly a worker in iron—*un feron*, from *fer*, iron, from Latin *ferrum*. Nobody actually knows who she was, or even if Leonardo was the artist. That style of headband, with a jewel in the middle of the forehead, came to be known as a *ferronnière*, considered very stylish for a long time."

"I think I'll make one for myself," Hannah said. "It's so pretty."

"You'd look beautiful in one," Yves told her.

"*Aww*," she said, appreciating his flattery.

They kissed, and Leonardo's famous lady seemed to be smiling with them across the room. The *Mona Lisa* had that effect on everyone in the world who saw her. Hannah wondered what Claudette Vervain knew, and intended to find out.

As another startling little side fact, Hannah noticed that the *Mona Lisa* also seemed to be wearing a ferronnière across her forehead, without a jewel. It was the fine border of a barely visible veil.

At least she had accomplished one thing by taking the day off, and dragging Yves away from his work. She'd found a clue that would lead her to Claudette Vervain, her father's lost love.

৪০ • ೮੪

As they stood together, leaning over the stone wall that overlooks the Seine in front of the Musée du Louvre, at the Quai des Tuileries, Yves looked a bit grim. "I won't give up so easily."

She punched him lightly, fondly, in the ribs. "Thank you."

He put his long arm protectively around her shoulder and back. "We will get to the bottom of it."

She held her hands against his side, as if his ribs were a pillow. She snuggled her cheek against the warmth of his body in his sweater. "You are my hero."

"Not a hero," he said fiercely in her ear. "Just a lucky guy to have found you."

"*Aww*," she intoned again, not for the first time that day. "You are my rock star. You are going to sell millions of videos and become the next famous producer."

He laughed. "I'd settle for being the next Yves."

"You are my Yves."

"Then I am already rich and famous."

"You and me, babe."

"You and me," he said devoutly as they became probably the billionth young couple to kiss avidly in Paris near the Seine by the Quai des Tuileries or a hundred similarly romantic places while boats passed on the river, trees rustled in a summery breeze, and blossoms fell like snow around them.

Image: *La Belle Ferronnière*, Leonardo Da Vinci, c. 1490-96
Courtesy Livio Andronico, Creative Commons, Wikimedia

10. Seeking Claudette Vervain

Hannah and Yves inquired at the information desk in the main building, and were directed to the Louvre administrative offices near the pyramid and the Carrousel.

After an initial greeting with a desk clerk, they were ushered into a comfortable office. A manager named Amélie Tournesol asked them to sit down before her wide desk on which sat semi-orderly stacks of papers and books. Madame Tournesol was small, blonde, and smartly dressed in a dark-blue suit with skirt and navy-blue medium heels. She seemed to have to raise her chin to speak over the edge of her desk. Hannah wished there was a crank of some sort to pump up her chair so Madame Tournesol would seem taller. Anyway, Mme Tournesol projected an air of interest, authority, and curiosity. "Where did you come across that name?" she asked. "I cannot find anything in our current employee or curatorial files. I have a researcher looking into it since you called it to my attention."

Yves rose respectfully, approached the vast desk, and showed her the brochure.

Madame Tournesol said in a dry humor: "I will need a microscope. I can have one sent up."

Hannah concurred. "I had to hold it up this way and that way to make out the fine print."

Madame Tournesol nodded. "I've sent someone out to research our older records. Let's wait a few moments. So in the meantime, tell me about your visit to the Louvre. Are you enjoying it?"

"Of course," said Yves proudly. "What Parisian would not be proud and happy?"

"*D'accord*," said Mme. Tournesol. "And you, *mademoiselle*, you are *Américaine*?"

"Oui, Madame," Hannah answered in her by now passably fluent French.

Mme. Tournesol raised a pleased eyebrow, and they continued a nice conversation for several minutes. In today's universal world, not surprisingly, Madame Tournesol's brother was a physician practicing in Boston, Massachusetts, and she had a sister married to a college professor in Berlin.

About ten minutes into all this polite conversation, Mme. Tournesol's desk phone warbled, and she picked up. It was clearly a conversation continued from a while earlier. She nodded as she exchanged brief phrases with the researcher in the stacks who had called: *Içi...oui...alors...*

When she was done, she hung up. She folded her hands together over her folded knees and said: "Good news and bad news." Seeing Yves and Hannah's expectant faces, she said: "The good news is that we have found records of a Mademoiselle Claudette Vervain, a master's degree candidate in History at the Sorbonne University here in Paris, what it was at that time. The bad news is that Mlle Vervain was killed in a car crash in 1981, ending her research assistantship here at the Louvre. She was only twenty-eight years of age." Mme Tournesol's eyes and features radiated not only sympathy, but genuine sadness.

Hannah's heart sank. *Oh,my,god, more horrible stuff.*

"I am sorry," Mme Tournesol said. "I don't know much more. My researcher found a clipping from our newspaper *Le Figaro* at that time, in the obituary section, which someone inserted into Claudette Vervain's personnel file as they closed it out forever. She was in a car with her fiancé, a Monsieur Arnold Parivel of Brussels, age thirty, who also died instantly. He was driving at very high speed, under the influence of alcohol and cocaine, and crashed into a tree head-first on the Quai Voltaire on the Left Bank as they were coming from a party and going to another."

"She was studying?" Yves asked, probing for any information that might be extracted from between the lines somehow. Hannah sat with her arm through Yves' arm, understanding his investigative nature.

Mme Tournesol was entirely sympathetic. "A terrible loss, yes. What makes me sad is that she has nearly been forgotten here at the museum, as well as over at the university. My researcher made some phone calls and this is all the information we have."

"Was she working on a project here?"

"Yes." Mme Tournesol sat forward, put some dark-framed reading glasses on her nose, and looked at her computer screen to one side. "This is the information that was just sent to me. Claudette Vervain was working on her Master's thesis."

"And that was about?" Yves prodded.

"Leonardo da Vinci. Specifically, the paintings here in the Louvre. First and foremost, not surprisingly, *La Joconde*, the Smiling *Mona Lisa*." She raised her hands and dropped them. "That is all I have, I am sorry. We don't even have a manuscript from her. She must not have had time to put her notes together for a first draft as required by her faculty advisor at that time. A Professor Alphonse Brouillard, who died a quarter century ago after retiring and moving to his home in Provençe. He died around 1983 or so. All gone. No trace."

Interview over, Mme Tournesol politely but firmly rose. "I'm sorry I could not be of more assistance." She shook their hands with her small, firm grip, no nonsense.

Moving on.

11.   Bridge of Regret

Days passed, and Hannah didn't look at Journal II. Rob had Journal III with him in Frankfurt, which was the easily knowable summary of Dan Wilson's life with Nancy Everol, with whom he had brought the twins Rob and Hannah into the world.

During her evening studies, Hannah might pick up her magnifying glass and try to make sense of the erratic notes her Dad had made in Journal II, a sort of scattershot mosaic of moments and events in a very dark time in Heidelberg and Verlorenau, lasting not quite three years. That was a standard period of enlistment in the United States Army in the post-Vietnam era U.S. Army. Frau Jones had related salient points from Dan's stay. Hannah found it heartbreaking to open the yellowing, dried up pages and see her father's cryptic entries written in a variety of ballpoint pens.

And then...

She came back with her magnifying glass to hover over those opening pages. While the window stood lightly open, and the curtains stirred in a mild summer night breeze, Hannah studied the inside of the front cover (card stock, nothing remarkable, even stained yellow with some droplets of tears, or beers, or long ago coffee). Those were the Cold War years. That had been Dan Wilson's war. He and well over a million U.S. service members, joining a million West German troops and another million or more Allies including Canadians, Danes, Belgians, you name it... held the line against the Warsaw Pact and the Stalinist empire. Heidelberg had been, according to one of Dad's stray notes, only about twelve minutes away from reach by Soviet fighter-bombers stationed in East Germany or Poland. Luckily, the trigger had never been pulled.

Something odd about that penciled name and address: *Claudette Vervain, 45 Rue de la Belle Ferronière, Paris 75012.* For some reason, it looked different than the rest of the writing. It was the only entry in pencil, for one thing. It was a very hard lead that came across fine and faint. Almost as if a woman had written it. Was it possible that Claudette Vervain had written her name and address for him? But why? At this point, he had left her for Stana Chetko in Verlorenau, Heidelberg.

A page or two into the notebook, she found another puzzling entry. Its title, underscored for emphasis, was Bridge of Regret. It was written in his firm, flowing blue ink from an ordinary stick pen, maybe a Bic or the like. The writing was different from that in pencil, which started more and more to look like the writing of a woman as Hannah studied the journal.

What was this about a Bridge of Regret?

It said *Pont des Arts—Bridge of Regret, Paris 75001*. Now she knew there had been a real bridge where Dan and Claudette last saw each other during that heart-rending, tearful goodbye. It was the Pont des Arts, the Bridge of the Arts, considered by many to be the most beautiful in Paris. It was a *passerelle*, a foot bridge for pedestrians, not a traffic bridge. It straddled the First Arrondissement on the Right Bank, and the Seventh Arrondissement on the Left Bank. This passerelle led straight to the entrance portal of the Palace du Louvre on Quai du François Mitterand.

The date of that sad moment was even there: September 25, 1977.

Farewell, my love. This is the most painful moment of my life, and yet the happiest. I suffer great pain as I leave you on the bridge. Your look will haunt me for the rest of my life. Your face is filled with pain, and your eyes are stunned with disbelief that I would leave you for another woman who is pregnant with my child. I could have done like so many men, French or otherwise, and simply lied and left you hanging to figure things out in pain and loneliness. I am too honest, and I don't want you to suffer. I want you to move on, to find a man more suited to your passion and education. Go on, discover the greatest secret of Leonardo that we dreamed of uncovering. You are close, and you will be famous. I was not meant to be on that journey with you. Fate has a different journey outlined for me, which I will find out when I return to Heidelberg. A piece of my heart and soul stays here with you, but I have betrayed you and don't deserve any kindness or fond memories from you. I love you with all my heart, as much as my heart is torn for those other loves in Germany. Goodbye, my love, and best of luck in your quest to solve the riddle of the Smiling Woman. May you smile also.

It was a paragraph of thoughts, rambling, rather than an actual letter to someone, so Dan Wilson, a young soldier age about 27, had not signed it. At some point not long after, with a date simply indicated by the month in autumn 1977, Dan Wilson had added the next entry.

October 1977: wedding date at beginning of November. Stana starting to show. Inlaws awful as always. Chetko an asshole. I can't wait to ETS and take her home to Portland with the baby so we can start a new life together, away from this dark and horrible village.

After some drawings and doodlings of no apparent purpose, maybe just to pass time while drinking, the next entry read:

November 12: Married and scared. Doubts. Will things ever change?
Stana drunk, doesn't want a baby, says Chetko raped her as a child. What
have I gotten into here? And the new supervision at work is from hell: a
lieutenant with a low IQ and a huge ego, sociopath monster; and a top striper
who hates me and the United States and prays for a white-only South to rise
again in Jesus' name or some such stupid shit.

Wish I could run away to Paris, kneel before Clau, beg her to forgive me.
But I am trapped here, drinking too much, my old friends all left at their ETS,
as I should have, rather than sink into this nightmare. I have no new friends.
Not a soul to talk to. This was heaven, and has become hell. I was a fool. Now
all I have to live for is my ETS. Getting Stana out of here so she can become
real with herself; and raising a wonderful child in Oregon, free from this
Dark Forest.

The document trailed on from there, consisting of many entries probably
made while Daddy was drunk, maybe sitting in the Zum Forst with Frau
Jones, who became one of his only allies.

The baby died, Stana stayed, and Dan left alone to start life all over.

When Hannah couldn't stand it anymore, she put the magnifier down
sharply, slammed the journal shut, and hoped she would never again have to
look inside of it, which was like opening a door and looking into a hot,
blazing, blinding hell.

As Hannah sat gathering her breath and calming down, she fought tears.

At the same time, something tingled at her memory: *Paris 75012.* That
would be the Twelfth Arrondissement. She and Yves had driven past that
somber, gray address in the *douzième* or Twelfth upstream on the Seine. She
pulled close her computer and researched online maps. She began near Bercy
Village, in the general area where the Marne and Seine Rivers flow together
westward as one river (the Seine) through the center of Paris. Nothing jumped
out at her. It was a dead end, or so it seemed, until a phone call the next day—
surprise—from Madame Tournesol at the Louvre administration offices.

12. Lost World: Claudette Vervain

The land line rang as Hannah was getting ready for work the next day. She sat down, with one nylon stocking on and the other one as far up as her right ankle. "Hello?"

"*Mademoiselle Wilson?*"

"*Oui?*"

"AmélieTournesol at the Louvre. Hope I didn't catch you at a bad time."

"Just getting ready for work. How are you?"

"Fine. I have one more little piece of news."

"Oh wow. Anything would help."

The distant voice said: "I don't know how much this would help, but my researcher has found out that even though we can't locate any papers of Mademoiselle Vervain, we did find a record in a file belonging to the late Professeur Brouillard. It seems he made a note in his day book in 1981 that he was working with Miss Vervain on her dissertation, advising her. He had recommended that she unearth the notes of a Professeur Benjamin Wandrous dating fifty years earlier, in the 1930s. Professeur Wandrous was a scholar who happened to be Jewish. He had grown up in Berlin with Walter Benjamin, the famous author of *Les Passages*, which are about those early glassed-over streets or *passages* (galeries) of Paris, but really a history of the century before everything went up in smoke in the 20th Century. Walter Benjamin died trying to escape the Nazis, while Benjamin Wandrous was sent off to Drancy and then Auschwitz where he died as well. Dr. Wandrous' entire family were deported, and his notes and books were brought into one of the museum collections and then forgotten. Brouillard was the son of one of Dr. Wandrous' students, who was a professor of History at the Sorbonne. So what I can tell you is that if you wish, you can stop by the university library at the Pantheon, and I will send instructions for them to give you access to the files. I assume you read French?"

"Not very well, but I'll bring my boyfriend Yves."

"Oh yes, the tall, handsome Parisian. I'm jealous."

"I am flattered, Madame. Thank you so much."

She laughed warmly. "My pleasure, sweetheart. Take care, and call me if I can help you again."

Wow.

After ringing off, Hannah sat with her loose nylon in both fists as if she were about to strangle herself.

Ha! Another break, maybe. Or not. But it would be worth pursuing.

ଡ଼ • ଔ

She called Yves, who agreed to meet her at the Pantheon-Sorbonne University I (among a dozen campuses around greater Paris) in the Latin Quarter, that afternoon. She left work early and took the Métro from the skyscrapers of La Défense to the more stately Sixth Arrondissement with its many historic features like the Pantheon, the Luxembourg Gardens, and the sprawling campus. She walked the last few blocks to the decorative campus of History and Humanities in the rue Saint-Jacques. Yves was waiting for her on the sidewalk, and they linked arms and strode inside.

Going down a long, darkly glowing corridor that echoed with voices and footsteps from passing students and faculty, they came to one in a row of doors marked (on wavy, milky glass, in gilded lettering) *Recherches*. On a small plaque on the wall next to the door was printed information, in black lettering on white plastic, indicating that the matters researched within were of modern sensitivity, perhaps an understatement referring to the deportations of Jews and intellectuals by the Nazis during World War Two.

Inside, they stepped up to a high podium-like counter and waited until a middle-aged man in a dark suit greeted them. He introduced himself as Monsieur Pierre Bondie, manager of the archives for something or other. He was slim, small, and balding with thin gray hair combed back over a sun-browned and spotted scalp. His gray plastic-rimmed glasses looked outsized for his dimensions, and kept threatening to slip down his long nose. His English was impeccable, to Hannah's joy.

"Madame Tournesol called, and I have your information ready." He graciously showed them to a table behind the counter. There, under a wall sconce, augmented by the light of an antique brass table lamp, Hannah and Yves sat side by side as he opened what looked like a shoebox. He lifted out a file binder tied with a string (resembling a shoe string) and peeled the marbled-looking brownish cardboard stock covers aside to reveal a thick stack of yellowing, aging papers written thickly in fountain pen long ago. He sat with them for a few minutes, zealously guarding his documents while Yves carefully leaved through them a page at a time.

After Monsieur Bondie was satisfied that they were not going to destroy or steal the records, and went to other rooms to do other business, Yves remarked under his breath: "This is odd."

Hannah noticed the name Leonardo da Vinci as Yves spoke. "Yes, dear?"

Yves pointed his fingertips at some crude but orderly, neat looking drawings done in the same fading bluish fountain pen. "Looks like a moon, doesn't it?"

"Hah," she said. "Well, Leonardo was a world-class scientist. A jack of all trades, but most importantly a thinker. Maybe this was some astronomical work."

"I am trying to follow Professor Wandrous' notes. It's difficult, because he seems to write backwards, in code, and abbreviates a lot."

She offered: "So these were his private notes, intended for him to review at his leisure."

Yves shook his head. "These are notes and drawings made by Professor Brouillard." He flipped down into the middle of the stack of papers. The papers were of different dimensions, and types, and even cuts. Some pages were thick enough to be blotters with frayed, pulpy edges. Others were sharp enough to cut skin. "Look here." He pointed. "Wandrous' handwriting was blockier, and mostly written in pencil."

Hannah tapped her fingernail on a line of writing. "He's using a Number One lead. How odd. That's how the entry for Claudette Vervain was written in Daddy's journal."

"So there is a connection," Yves said.

"Yes, except Wandrous was at least thirty years dead when that entry was made by my Dad."

"So Wandrous didn't come back and write in your Dad's journal."

"Nope. So who did?"

Yves stared at her. "You know something I don't?"

"Just a guess." She pointed to her heart. "My gut. My heart."

He thought about it for a few minutes. "Let's make copies of all this if we can."

They consulted with Monsieur Bondie, who told them: "There will be a slight charge, just nominal. And I estimate it will take at least three days, but yes, we can provide you with copies. Madame Tournesol has already vouched for you, so your credentials are good." He escorted them back to the *recéption.* "You may call me in about two or three days and I will be glad to update you. You can pick up the copy or we can ship it to you."

"We'll pick it up," Hannah said. "Can't wait."

℘ • ℭ

Outside on the sidewalk, they stood uncertainly for a moment. "What do you want to do?" Yves asked as he shuffled his feet and had his hands in his pockets.

She gave him a friendly rap with the back of her fist. "We're not far from that address, the Rue de la Belle Ferronière. I have a feeling if we go back there and poke around, we might learn something."

He shook his head in affectionate amazement. "Being with you is an adventure. Come on, let's go. Maybe we can stop for a beer in the Bercy Village."

They linked arms and strode toward the nearest Métro station. "Wine, not beer. Sacrilege." She meant of course that Bercy was a wine warehousing district, now converted to a modern tourist attraction called Bercy Village. He laughed and gave her arm a slight tug. "So call me a heretic."

13. Claudette's Nephew

They stepped down in the Métro at Place Monge and rode eastward, crossing the Seine, past Bercy, and in the direction of the Avenue Daumesnil, Bel-Air, Rue de l'Alouette, near the Bois de Vincennes. From there, it was a ten minute walk further.

"Looks familiar," Yves said. "Last time, I was driving."

"Things always go by too fast when we drive."

They walked with crunching steps on cobblestones, through a short grayish-dark tunnel of unevenly cut stones, and into the square that was the Rue de la Belle Ferronière. It was less of a *rue* (street) than a *place* or even a *square*. Holding hands, they walked into the empty seeming courtyard.

"It does say *Rue* on the sign going into the tunnel," Yves said.

"It's just a courtyard. There's that No. 45 again." She stood pointing to the steel door with the straps and studs.

Behind them, a man's voice startled them. "*Bonjour.*"

As they turned, there was a tremendous splash of water, and they jumped back. But it was just a young man in shorts and a T-shirt, emptying a bucket of what looked like paint water into the heavy gutter grating in the center of the square.

"*Bonjour,*" Yves said.

The man, who was about thirty, stood looking at them expectantly somehow, as if he anticipated a conversation. He had short brown hair, a sort of edgy, triangular, bony face, and large brown eyes. He had fairly bad skin mottled with beard shadow, acne scars, and one or two oddly blue birthmarks.

"Do you speak English?" Hannah asked. She found herself almost yelling, which was the tendency of most people when speaking with someone through a language barrier; the idea that, if you yelled, they could understand you better. She stopped in embarrassment, and held the fingertips of one hand to her lips.

"A little," the man said. "You are *des Américains*?"

Yves was about to inform him huffily that he was not just French, but Parisian. Seeing that coming, Hannah put her hand out and stepped in front. "We are looking for a long-lost family member."

"Oh? Who is that?"

"Have you ever heard of a Claudette Vervain?"

Still looking surprised, the man brightened. "My aunt."

"She is deceased?" Hannah asked.

"Long ago. She was the sister of my mother, also deceased now." He pointed to No. 45. "We lived there. Now we rent it out to a Swedish family who are not home much. The father teaches at the Sorbonne. Chemistry or something. I don't know. I don't have university. I drive a taxi."

"Your English is wonderful," Hannah said.

He grinned. "Thank you. Taxi driving is a school of everything— politics, languages, how to tame wild animals."

"Dealing with the public," Hannah said, picking up on his metaphor. She tugged quietly at Yves' hand, to get him out of his funk and into the conversation.

"We are glad to meet you," Yves said.

La même. "Same here." The young man set his bucket down. He wiped his hands on his work-dirty T-shirt. "What makes you look for my aunt?"

"My father was a friend of hers," Hannah said.

"That was long ago. When?"

"Around 1977. Almost half a century ago."

"*Oui.* Before my time."

"Mine too," Hannah said. "My father loved her very much, I think. I am reading his old journals. He died not long ago."

"My mother told me about her sister. Very sad. So frustrating. She was disappointed in a love affair, maybe with your father, and started going out with a Belgian who drank too much and one day killed them both with the car crash. You know." He banged his fists together. *Boum.*

"She was a brilliant woman," Yves said.

"What is your name?" Hannah asked.

"François Bergier. My mother's maiden name was Vervain, like her sister."

"Voilà," Hannah exclaimed.

"Vervain," François corrected.

"The game," Yves said.

"Ah yes, I've heard of it. Our family name long ago is Italian. You know Napoléon Bonaparte turned the world upside down. We are all still recovering from that."

"Too many tyrants for any possible recovery," Yves said with a dark laugh. "So we must drink beer."

François laughed. "Now you are speaking my language. Can I offer you wine or beer?"

"Delighted," Yves said, though Hannah poked him in the ribs with her elbow, not wanting to intrude too much, too fast.

They trooped inside his house. He was that rare person: a young, single man who owned a house, or actually almost a small block, in the city, and rented parts of it out at presumably a healthy profit. No university, as he said, but a head for staying ahead of things.

A pretty Mediterranean-looking girl or young woman entered, with caramel skin color, glossy black hair, lively dark eyes. She wore a traditional housecoat (gray, did not show stains much, covered with tiny pretty little flowers). Shapely and vivacious, she carried Vichy soda water bottles under both arms, and two more full bottles, one in each hand. *Bonjour*, she exclaimed while heading to an open window, overlooking a cool and shady side yard full of vines and bushes. She lined up the bottles on a wooden sill, where they would stay cool.

"My girlfriend, Asmá," François introduced the pretty girl, to whom he said: "Visitors, looking for my aunt Claudette."

"Oh," Asmá said. "A few years too late."

Judging by her olive color, she must be *pied-noir* or outright North African, Hannah thought; either a child of returned French settlers, or else native Algerian. The young woman patiently explained that her name was a French variation of its Arabic source, Asmaa, stress on the final syllable.

They all sat at a large square wooden table with a blue and white checked cloth. In the center was a basket with what looked like Asmá's knitting—two or three balls of light lavender wool, some needles, and a knitted square. "Baby?" Hannah asked.

"For my little nephew," Asmá said proudly. She rubbed her flat stomach. "Not yet." She looked at François impishly.

He gave a faint shrug. "No hurry. Take life a day at a time."

"I like that philosophy," Yves said.

Asmá put her hand over François' and said: "I like him. He is patient."

"I like you too," François said. "You are sharp, like a stone."

"So step on me," Asmá said, shaking him by the hand.

François laughed. "You see that we two get along well."

"So what brings you to our little *ruelle*?" Asmá asked. Her last name was Boussouf, as Hannah could see from a high school diploma hanging on a kitchen wall. Probably *métisse*, Hannah thought, a mixed race woman, Arab or Berber or whatever. Very beautiful and lively. Part of the modern Parisian landscape, for all of its blemishes and beauties: cosmopolitan, tolerant, colorful, interesting, full of promise for the future —*so cool*, Hannah thought.

Asmá rose and got glasses, and poured everyone a half glass of red wine. She sat *gamine* on a stool, with one pretty smooth café-au-lait leg under the other. Her hair was cut page-boy style, shiny black, and slightly raised in the rear for a young, boyish effect that emphasized her feminine prettiness. Hannah rarely got girl-crushes, but Asmá was just adorable. A small, perfect nose. She didn't know François from—oops, yes she did, a distant part of Daddy's love story—she was just now glowing with happiness for François, who seemed like such a nice young guy. Crawling with emotion, she stuck her arm through Yves' arm, and gave him a dreamy shake. He patted her hand to comfort her, assuming she was probably emotional about her aunt. He trapped her hand in his, and pulled it close to his ribs. Had she been a cat, Hannah would have purred.

Meanwhile, François got a distant, longing look in his eyes. "She died before I was born, Aunt Claudette. I have seen old videos of her at the beach at Deauville with my mother, Clothilde Vervain, and my grandparents and cousins and so forth. They were all very happy together. It was a good family."

"Still is," Asmá said, shaking him boyishly by the shoulders.

François sank into a reverie, seeming to collapse inwardly a bit at memories, sadness, melancholy, things lost, loved ones gone. "I am told that my aunt was studying paintings at the Louvre by famous artists."

"Leonardo da Vinci," Yves prodded.

François shrugged. "Yes, something like that. Not my *métier*." (Translated, Hannah knew, that meant in English something like 'above my pay grade'). "But I greatly respect smart people like my aunt. My mother was a nurse; not bad either."

Through a glass of wine, and a warm haze of new friendship, they bantered and joked.

Something nevertheless darkened François' look slightly, making him look puzzled, until finally he snapped his fingers. "Of course. The *Americain*. My mother said he broke Aunt Claudie's heart. She then ran around with this Belgian asshole who got them both killed."

Asmá patted his hand. "Poor man. Relax, they are all in heaven now. We have our own lives to get on with."

"You are my angel," François said sincerely.

Asmá's eyes rose full of light and mischief, and her pretty mouth pursed in a smile. "I'll be your love any time. But not Angel, please, wait until we are in heaven."

"Sorry," François said. "Life is good. No death wish."

Hannah started telling him a little bit about her father, and the reasons compelling her searches.

"You want to learn more," François said questioningly.

"All that I can," she said. "For my twin brother in Frankfurt as well."

"I may have something to show you," François said slowly, biting his lip. "You cannot take it with you, but I will show you. Maybe we'll make copies, eh?"

He left the kitchen, and returned a few minutes later with a woman's canvas bag. It was a pretty satchel—wheat-colored, woven in a hard flaxy grain, with a huge, multi-colored pastel (pink blue yellow green) flower with stem and leaves crocheted on its side.

As he put the bag on the table, he said confessionally: "You are not the first to come here in the last few days."

That's why you looked so strange, so surprised yet not surprised, Hannah thought, remembering how he had looked at them after splashing the water into the gutter.

"There was a blonde woman, about two days ago."

Asmá shrugged her shoulders, making a comical face. "I think he was hallucinating."

"I did see her. I spoke with her."

Asmá made a face of surrender. "If you say so, my love."

François said: "She had golden-blonde hair down to her shoulders, and a plain stylish sort of dress women in Paris wear to go shopping when they really mean business."

As he spoke, there was a strange feeling inside Hannah. It was as if a light were shining, and she saw herself at Dad's funeral back in Oregon. Such a woman stood in the crowd of mourners—silent, with sunglasses, and a raincoat, hands in her pockets, looking there but not there.

A voice in her head said—as time slowed to a glue pace, and François seemed frozen in the act of reaching into the bag—a mature woman's voice said in a measured, self-assured, comforting tone: "Everything is as it was meant to be, don't worry. It will all turn out for the best."

The momentary vision was over, and François pulled *Journal I* from his bag. "The *Americain* and my aunt, they put together this scrapbook." He laid on the table before Hannah a thick object, almost more of a photo album or scrapbook, rather than a notebook like the other two notebook journals.

Still dreamy, Hannah felt as though she were staring at the book through whirling dust motes, the way a shaft of sunlight will cut through a closed window and shed its golden light into a dusky stairwell, trapping tiny dust particles that whirl around like confused insects in a fluid, turbulent dance.

Asmá said brightly: "I have an idea. Let me go get my camera. It's a digital, *trop de* megapixels, and well have as many good quality pictures as you wish."

"Perfect," François said. "And I can put them on a disk or up in the cloud so you can download them when you wish. And besides, we are going to be here. We are not going away. So you are welcome to return any time you wish for another look." He put his hand over Hannah's, leaned forward to look with earnest love into her eyes, and said sincerely: "We are like family, *non*?"

Yves nodded slowly, looking a bit overwhelmed and uncertain, but reluctantly willing to buy into the agreement being forged.

"That means so much to me," Hannah whispered.

She put her hands on it, as she had over the previous journal at the tavern in the hills and forest above Heidelberg. So here it was, her father's missing Journal I. *The last one, but is it the final one? Or are there yet more chapters to be found?*

She whispered, more to herself than to Yves, and just as much to Rob: "Now we have Journals III, II, and I. A long, good life; preceded by a marriage made in hell; preceded by a slice of heaven let go at a Bridge of Regret in Paris. There has to be something more."

The journey was not yet over, she knew in her heart. The really wild ride was just beginning.

Part Three

Journal I

Lest They Be Angels

Heidelberg 1975-1977

14. Journal I At Last (Happy)

A young soldier named Daniel Wilson, from Oregon, had arrived in Germany in autumn of 1975. His entry dates, recorded in a variety of ballpoint pen colors, were often hastily scribbled, hard to read, and sometimes just cryptic remarks about dropping off his uniform at the PX for cleaning, or remembering a dental appointment, or working late at his file clerk duties to catch up.

By autumn 1975, the newly arrived young clerk was already taking weekend trips. He had studied German in high school and during his interrupted college studies in Portland. He had a lively and curious mind, and a fondness for artsy subjects like History, Literature, and languages.

Along with the more intelligent and flexible of his fellow enlisted men and women, he liked taking some of the many tours offered through the Armed Forces Exchange. His scribblings noted a one-day tour of Frankfurt, a two-day with a hotel stay in Cologne, and longer visits including several weekend jaunts to Paris. The U.S. military had some cooperative programs with the West German army, like for attending hot football games (meaning what the U.S. called soccer). He went to one such game in Dortmund (Borussia Dortmund versus Arminia Hannover) and on another occasion in Darmstadt (City Team versus Frankfurt). On both football occasions he came home with his friends, hung over for days from drinking world-class beer from the barrel in festival tents, and resumed his tasls as a personnel file clerk and the usual round of usually 24-hour duty roster assignments. Living in the barracks at the time, he also had a regular Monday morning inspection to prepare for.

Then, in autumn 1976, he began writing notes about Paris. From Heidelberg, on Friday evenings, he could take a short train ride on the Bundesbahn to Mannheim, where he'd switch to another DB train carrying hundreds of French soldiers home to France for the weekend. The fare was not expensive. He never needed a passport traveling anywhere in Europe, but showed his SOFA card (Status of Forces Agreement) to police and customs agents anywhere he went within NATO. That was simply a little laminated dollar-green card with his photo on it, and his status as a U.S. soldier serving in NATO. It was the size of his library card or driver's license back home, and stayed in his wallet. Much of western part of West Germany was once again in the French zone of occupation after World War Two, as it had been after the First World War. The French had garrisons up and down the Rhine River, and their troops liked to go home for a visit as often as possible. The Friday evening express from Koblenz to Paris was, in effect, a troop train, though not designated as such. Dad'a journal called it a 'troop express' with funny faces drawn alongside. His Journal I entries were full of happy caricatures from a young man having the time of his life in Europe, whereas the Journal II entries were dour and tear-stained; and the Journal III entries of his later civilian life were sober but happy recitations of family events, an occasional season's prayer (Christmas, Easter), and photos pasted in of the babies (Rob, Hannah) with their mom, a smiling and pretty young brunette.

Dan bought a used car cheaply from another soldier leaving on ETS, so then he could go on weekend jaunts with his buddies all over—to Brussels, to Munich, to Amsterdam, and many other cool places. If you were scheduled for 24 hours on duty Saturday or Sunday, and needed to go to Paris for a day, you swapped duties with someone at another date, or paid someone twenty-five bucks to take your place.

West Berlin was a different matter, being isolated in the heart of Communist East Germany. You didn't just drive there on the Autobahn. Instead, he did take a Berlin Tour by train, courtesy of U.S. Army Europe, which was eye-opening. In one entry, he mentioned standing on the Western side and looking across the no man's land between the two walls at his Warsaw Pact counterpart, a young soldier who stared back with binoculars, took a photograph for some reason, and then slammed the blinds shut. In the no man's land were barbed wire, land mines above or below ground, and sometimes starving dogs running on patrol looking for human meat to bite into (those fleeing from East to West). The buried landmines all along the FRG/DDR borders were meant to kill innocent people by stealth, while the above-ground mines on short steel poles were mockingly advertised with signs that told fleeing families they were about to be blown up by the Democratic People's Republic of Germany.

Dan also mentioned Soviet soldiers and officers inspecting the passenger manifest on the U.S. Army train (which ran as an act of defiance between Free World territory in West Berlin, through hostile territory in East Germany, and back to West Germany or the Federal Republic of Germany (FRG). As the train clattered slowly on antiquated tracks through East Germany (the same tracks that had carried millions of victims to concentration camps in the east), the train passed over deep trenches lit garishly by anti-aircraft searchlights. Stationed down below were VOPO and East German army snipers, ready to shoot and kill any fleeing refugees who might be clinging to the bottoms of the carriages occupied by visiting U.S.

soldiers in their best Class A uniforms. VOPO were the East German Volkspolizei, or People's Police, who still wore old-fashioned 1800s black leather police caps (not to be confused with *Pickelhauben*, or spiked helmets, worn long-ago by the Kaiser-era German soldiers).

The young Dan Wilson living and working and partying in Europe would usually save himself a night's hotel in Paris by taking a bottle of wine along on that Friday evening French troop express, sitting on a coach as far from the carousing, singing, boozing French soldiers with their deep voices. He'd drink his wine either from the bottle or from whatever plastic container was available from the onboard vendor. He'd fall asleep by ten p.m in his seat, with his head lolling against the window as the train rocked from West Germany into France through the night, and wake by dawn at the Gare de l'Est in Paris; a cup of black coffee, croissant, cheese, and ham at the train station restaurant would drive away any cobwebs—including one occasion, when he dreamed of boisterous French soldiers sneaking toward his compartment and bursting into a loud rendition of *Alouette, Gentille Alouette*. All in good fun.

Hannah noticed a change, a growing maturity in her father's notes. Sometime in autumn 1975, he met a young woman named Claudette Vervain in Paris. As best Hannah could figure out, Dan had gone to one of his favorite hotels, an Ibis or a Novotel in the suburbs. It was one of those adventuresome, determined trips he sometimes took by himself, when nobody else was willing or able to go. As a junior enlisted, he had several extra duty days a month, like being CQ Runner for the Charge of Quarters NCO in one of the barracks, or duty driver for FOD (Field Officer of the Day), which sometimes involved driving to Frankfurt to pick up a soldier being assigned to Heidelberg. All this was noted, sometimes tediously, in Dan's journal. Most U.S. Army troops came into USAREUR through Rhein-Main Air Force Base in Frankfurt, from where military buses ferried them to the grim, red-brick old Gutleut Kaserne downtown near the main railroad station (Hauptbahnhof). Gutleut Kaserne was a self-contained time capsule, a city block big, surrounded by barbed wire atop tall red-brick walls. It was patrolled by its own resident Military Police (MP) unit, typical of the Army's pragmatic (Dan added in the margin, underlined several times: *cynical*?) expectations of sometimes treating its own troops as inmates . Dan's margin scribbles included: *All part of that Cold War charm. When will they turn on the lights again in Europe?*

80 ● ○3

For about a year (1976-1977), Dan's journal entries grew less detailed and more obviously ecstatic. He pasted in a few pictures of an elegant young brunette (Claudette Vervain) standing with him in various places around Paris. How happily they smiled in photos taken by a passer-by for them. They stood before the Louvre (where she was doing her Master's thesis on a project involving some obscure aspect of Leonardo da Vinci's *Mona Lisa*).

There was even a shot of them on the *passerelle* crossing the Seine, the Pont des Arts, which he would forever call the Bridge of Regret. In other photos, they sat in restaurants in the Marais or the Latin Quarter with loving family members—a far cry from the *Vogelscheuchen*, scarecrows, as he already called his frightening peasant future in-laws in Verlorenau.

Not unexpectedly, Dan and Claudette spent many hours touring the usual hot spots as if they had never been to Paris before, including Arc de Triomphe d'Etoile, the Eiffel Tower, and some of those haunting glass-and-iron covered *passages* resembling early shopping malls already in the late 1700s and early 1800s.

The scrap book of Asmá and François went on for at least twenty pages, telling the story of Dan & Claudette's happy year 1976 to 1977 before he left her for Stana at the Bridge of Regret.

ഔ • ൝

Hannah spent two hours on the phone with her brother in Frankfurt, discussing the contents of Journal I. Rob agreed that there was something, somehow, yet missing. Neither he nor Hannah could explain this feeling. It was an instinct, rising from deep in the heart, like a ghostly cry for daylight. During that call, Rob announced that he and Elise were going to drive down to Paris for a three-day weekend.

Yves offered to put them up in a spare bedroom in his apartment in the Rue de Maspéro. His studio was going through a bit of a funk, and he wasn't making as much income as he would have liked. A wealthy relative, cousin twice removed of his mother, let him stay in a basement studio apartment whose slit-window looked up onto a busy sidewalk. The rent was cheap, the facilities were modern and clean, and he had a king-sized bed in which he and Hannah could tumble.

Hannah began spending more of her time there than in her own little digs in Autueil, a half hour's walk away, or a ten minute drive on a good day. And Yves' cousin had a three car garage in an adjoining *pâté* or block, to which Yves was able to get access for his car and a van full of studio equipment. What he needed was his own permanent studio, he said, but that would come. He was waiting for the next big pop music act to come along. Meanwhile, he and Hannah made for a young, attractive, energetic, fun loving couple to be seen strolling on rainy, neon-lit boulevards among the tourists and bustling locals.

She was having fun, so Hannah thought at times, like Daddy should have kept on having instead of his nightmare near Heidelberg. Even this ongoing grind of reading Dad's journals was wearying. Good thing Yves was a born investigator, and relished the hunt. So they were pleasantly surprised and excited when word came from University I Pantheon that their copy of the Wandrous papers from 1937 was ready for pickup.

15.   Package from Pantheon

Rob and Elise drove down from Frankfurt. They stopped in Luxembourg-ville for an early dinner with her family, the Gillen. Next she heard, Rob was phoning her from his car en route near Epernay. They were going to pick up a few bottles of Champagne and be in Paris by about seven in the evening. It was late summer, and the sky would be light out until well after ten p.m. at their latitutude north of the Equator. It was later than what Rob and Hannah were used to in Portland; longer days, shorter nights in summer but longer nights, shorter days in winter the higher up in latitude you went from the Equator toward the Arctic Circle; just another of many things to get used to, often surprising, for U.S. ex-pats in Europe.

Hannah took Friday off from work to be with Rob, Yves, and Elise.

Feeling well rested—unaware of the disturbing discovery yet to come—they ate a hearty breakfast with coffee, eggs and ham, brioches with butter and strawberry jam, at an outdoor corner restaurant near the small park in the Rue Galande, Paris 75005 (Fifth Arrondissement in the Latin Quarter, Left Bank of the Seine).

It was a mixed day—sunny, breezy late summer and balmy early autumn day. An occasional stray shower and a snap of wind freshened things up. The leaves still looked green, but the first hints of yellow and red were starting to be visible. There was a wonderful lightness in the air. After lunch, they went for a leisurely stroll, the two couples each arm in arm. *We look so much like we belong together,* Hannah thought with a warm thrill. Family again, *at last.*

It was a good, solid feeling, after losing her parents, selling their childhood home in Portland, and slowly establishing roots here in a Europe whose denizens not often readily hospitable to strangers. She found most Europeans to be more reserved, though they could be just as warm when they opened up (sometimes reluctantly).

They strolled toward the Seine, and stopped at Shakespeare & Co. The original namesake 1919 landmark bookstore, relocated 1922 to the 6th Arrondissment, was a haunt of Ernest Hemingway and his wives, along with many famous authors from the U.S., U.K., and elsewhere in the 1920s era of the Lost Generation, including James Joyce, F. Scott Fitzgerald, and many others). Sylvia Beach's famous store in the Sixth Arrondissement closed during the Nazi occupation. The current store, in its Fifth Arrondissement location, was launched in the 1950s, and renamed Shakespeare & Company as a tribute to.

The man who revived it was a former U.S. soldier named George Whitman, who followed Sylvia Beach's philosophy of generosity and hospitality, especially for destitute writers adrift in Paris and struggling to write great literature while caging the next cup of coffee. Whitman's best years coincided with another post-war lost generation, the 1950s Beats, including or embracing more broadly a wide range of poets and artists like Allen Ginsberg, Anaïs Nin, Henry Miller, Lawrence Durrell, and Lawrence Ferlinghetti. Whitman died at age 98 in his apartment above the bookstore. His daughter and only child Sylvia, born 1981, took over the operation, and a coffee shop was added next door. Hannah got a strange feeling as she pointed out to her companions a famous, hand-lettered sign over an inside door within the cramped bookstore:

Be not inhospitable to strangers, lest they be angels in disguise.

The quote is attributed to the Irish poet and Nobel Literature laureate William Butler Yeats (1865-1939), but dates to the Christian Testament (Epistle to the Hebrews 13:2).

Hannah felt a chill as she stepped back, while reading that famous legend. At that moment, she accidentally bumped into an attractive golden-blonde woman, with warm pale skin, who wore a light custard-yellow summer dress wind-borne at the knees; below that, bare legs, black high heels; her bare arms wrapped around a long glossy black leather purse with gilded snaps. The woman's bare hands looked pink and clean, her long fingers tipped with perfect violet-enameled nails. She wore a delicate golden Tissot wristwatch, and a slightly clunky bracelet of amber rocks on the other wrist held together by a white elastic. The woman looked familiar, somehow.

Excusez-mois, Hannah said in her best French. "I'm so sorry."

"Don't worry," said the woman in perfect U.S. English. "Everything will be fine." Seeing a fellow *Américaine* in a place like this did not surprise Hannah, since she'd met, passed, bumped into, been bumped by, or exchanged greetings with at least ten thousand tourists from every state of the Union.

"Lovely day," Hannah said awkwardly as she regained her balance after brushing against the stranger's long, warm, slender, sort of athletically firm body.

"A little rain in Paris makes for a charming atmosphere." The woman slipped a pair of dark sunglasses in tortoise shell amber frames onto her nose, disguising her striking greenish-amber pupils, and strode determinedly past

Hannah on strong legs, vanishing in a blot of blinding water-dissolved sunshine that poured like mercurial light through the shop's windows.

ℬ • ℭ

"Who is your friend?" Yves asked as he took Hannah protectively by the elbow.

"Some tourist from the U.S.A.," Hannah said in a peppery tone. She changed topics. "Ready to wander over and pick up our package at the university from Monsieur Bondie?" She turned to Rob, who stood arm in arm with Elise, who was studying some French-language magazines on a table. "Rob?"

"I heard you. Yeah," her sibling said, "we don't all have to troop over there."

"It's a few blocks," Hannah said.

"About a fifteen minute hike," Yves said.

"I have a suggestion," Hannah said. "Yves, why don't you take Elise down to the Quai de Montebello for a little fresh air, and relax a while?"

"I'd love that," Elise said, hands in her pockets, with her purse dangling by its strap. Her dress was so typically Elise, a quiet and elegant milk-chocolate knit with softly pearly, coin-sized buttons up and down. It was almost a big, tube-shaped, adventuresome sweater she could jam her hands into, with a fun denim skirt peeking out underneath. That, and white sports shoes for walking, some light silver jewelry, and a white *couronne* across the front of her straight, smooth chestnut hair—Rob's beloved looked right at home in Paris.

Hannah purred into Yves' embrace. "You will be my gentleman for a little while?"

"Of course," he whispered dramatically. "I will be lost without you, but this mermaid of Luxembourg will provide me with the light of her charms."

They laughed a silly, innocent laugh. The mermaid reference was to the famous mermaid Melusine of Luxembourgeois legend, who a thousand years ago had married Count Sigefroi. Melusine was beautiful, and asked only of her husband to be left alone for a few hours each week. She would lock herself in a private apartment overlooking the valley that surrounds the Old City, not far from Elise's family home and garden over the same valley. One day, curious what Melusine might be doing locked in that cliff apartment, Sigefroi tiptoed up and peeked through the keyhole. He was shocked to see his beloved wife in her bath, splashing around with a huge pair of mermaid fins instead of her usual womanly legs. With her keen senses, not to mention her sense of honor, she cried out in shock that he was spying on her—and slipped out through the window. She vanished in thin air above the lower city, and was never seen again.

"You won't slip away on me, will you?" Rob asked as he gave Elise a little nuzzle.

She laughed delightedly, glowing with love, and shook her head. "If you see me grow fins all of a sudden, watch out!"

Rob laughed warmly. With a final wave goodbye, Rob and Hannah strode away toward the Quai du Montebello. Yves and Elise waved and strolled off in the direction of the Île-de-la-Cité, probably to take a walk into the looming Notre Dame de Paris cathedral, or to the ancient Roman archeological digs nearby, or maybe lean on a stone wall overlooking the Seine current coming toward them, carrying myriad dapples of sunlight in its waves, by the Quai of Flowers at the Saint-Louis Bridge.

ଔ • ଔ

Rob and Hannah had an uneventful, brisk walk south toward the Pantheon.

Monsier Bondie was out to lunch, but a pleasant young secretary received them with friendly greetings. She was a slightly chubby young blonde with dimples in her smiling cheeks, and light glasses of a watery blue shade. She intoned: *Bonjour, votre paquet des papiers est prêt.*

Reaching below the counter, she handed over the package, which resided in a wrinkly white paper bag. Rob and Hannah stepped close to accept it with expressions of gratitude.

ଔ • ଔ

At that moment, has Hannah's hands reached across the desk and touched the paper, something came over her. It was indefinable, as if the ground had slightly shifted, or the light changed from one subtle beer-colored shade to another, or two different grades of caramel-colored glass.

She looked at Rob, who regarded her with startled eyes.

"Did you feel something?" she asked.

Rob shook his head with a confused look. Had there not been a blonde woman standing before them a few seconds ago?

The young African-French student in a blue blazer, who had handed the package over, nodded efficiently. It was clear he had work to return to, and would not linger with them. "Is everything all right?"

Hannah felt as if she were standing in a bath of light-amber glue.

Rob's voice sounded strangely droning beside her, as he took the package. "Yes, I think so."

"Have a great day then," said the young man.

Something is wrong, Hannah thought. *Something just changed. A big something, but what?*

ଔ • ଔ

"Fresh air," Rob said as they left the university building and crossed a square of green lawns and fragrant thickets.

"Let's go sit and have a look in the package," Hannah said.

"I could use a beer."

"You men and your beers. Make that two."

They walked back in the direction of the Seine along the rue des Carmes. Rob looked impatient suddenly, or driven. "We'll have our beers down by the river. Let's join the others. It's only another ten minutes" They crossed the intersection at the rue des Écoles.

"All right." Hannah slipped her arm through his for steadying.

"You feel okay?"

"I'm not sure. Yes. I think so."

"I felt sort of odd myself," he said. "I thought my stomach was going to twist around."

"Something we ate," she guessed.

They came to the Boulevard Saint-Germain, did a quick dog-leg across the Place Maubert with its little copse of trees, and continued at a brisk, now urgent pace north along the rue Frédéric-Sauton which brought them to the narrow, green streets in the Sorbonne Quartier, emerging at the Seine from the rue du Haut Pavé.

Soon, they approached the Quai de Montebello. There was the Seine ahead, with the Gothic structures of the Notre Dame de Paris cathedral floating in silent beauty and power from another age.

They turned left on the Quai de Montebello, with the Notre Dame looming beautifully on their right across the water. The little Square Viviani park was about to float past on their left. As they walked, Rob kept trying his cell phone. "Elise is not answering."

Hannah did the same, with similar result. "No word from Yves. Do you suppose they eloped together?"

Rob shook his head. "She is too much in love with my U.S. barbecue when I grill for the family in Luxembourg. No, she would not run off on me, even with a handsome movie star like Yves."

"Oh Rob, I'm worried. Stop joking."

"Just trying to stay light, Sis."

"I know. I'm sorry. I am such a worry-wart."

"Let's just grab a table at Shakespeare and wait for them. Maybe their cell phones fell in the river when they bent over to look at the fishes."

८० ● ८४

They walked by the little park called Square Viviani, where Hannah often liked to come, and cut into the cobblestoned side street Rue de la Bûcherie. There was Shakespeare & Co, solid as could be. On the corner of

St. Julien le Pauvre (Saint Julian the Poor) was the Shakespeare & Company Café adjacent to the bookstore.

"I feel at home here already," Hannah said.

"More like a pair of lost sheep,' Rob muttered.

He went inside to get two coffees, while she sat outside. She pulled out the documents copied for them by Monsieur Bondie. Rob strode out minutes later carrying a takeout coffee cup in each hand. He slid onto the bench beside her at one of the little umbrella-covered tables by the café door.

On the sidewalk in front of the little bookstore was a green Wallace Fountain, one of those cast-iron drinking installations about the size of a small person, which stood at many locations across Paris. Sir Richard Wallace, an English aristocrat caught up in the destruction of Paris during the Franco-Prussian War and the Paris Commune of 1871, had helped in the reconstruction of Paris by providing drinking fountains for the population. The fountains were now part of the landscape, dating from the industrial iron age of the late 1800s that had given the world the Eiffel Tower and many other iron structures.

The atmosphere was faintly uneasy around them, as if the air had a different chemistry, while they sipped their coffees and studied the papers. Sitting side by side, they leafed through one page after another. In all, there must be about a hundred pages, she estimated. Most of them were hand-written notes by Benjamin Wandrous or his assistants more than eighty years ago, in the 1930s, before the German invasion and the occupation of Paris that lasted from 1940 to 1944 when the Allies drove the Germans out.

Hannah said: "Looks like Claudette Vervain and her mentor were deciphering Wandrous' notes." She pointed to newer notes in the margins alongside Wandrous' crabbed writing.

Rob said: "Your French is a lot better than mine. I'm better at German these days."

She nodded, preoccupied. "There are notes here with important looking underscores, mentioning the *Mona Lisa* several times."

"The painting?"

"The one in the Louvre," she said. "I wonder what François would make of this."

"Your new friend?"

"Yeah. With the adorable girlfriend. You'll love them. Wanna go visit?"

"Sure, why not? Yves and Elise will contact us when they are ready." He sounded hopeful rather than definite. He tried the phone once more as he rose, with no luck. "It seems to be working, but they aren't answering." He shook the little charcoal-colored device.

"Let me try mine," she said. She raised her *tablette* and pressed her pre-dialed home number. It rang several times, and then a robotic voice said in French that the number was not in service.

That can't be, Hannah thought. *How weird.*

They rose and walked to the Quai de Montebello, where they hailed a passing taxi.

Traffic was average, and they found themselves in the little cobblestoned alley named Rue de la Belle Ferronière. As the taxi drove away, Rob and Hannah stood side by side with Rob holding the paper sack under one arm.

Hannah led the way into that short, shady tunnel with stone blocks above and cobblestones under their feet, in the 12th Arrondissement.

"Feels a bit strange," Hannah said.

"Interesting place," Rob said. "Paris is full of these little surprises. So it dead-ends on a courtyard?"

"Strange," Hannah said, slowing her stop and holding out a hand to caution him. "Something is different." She walked a few more hesitant steps and saw the number 45 on the outside wall, next to the steel door, which was closed. She felt a trifle relieved. "Maybe it's just me. I'm imagining things." She made a fist and rapped on the steel door with her knuckles.

They waited.

Somewhere in her memory, a woman's voice told Hannah: "Everything will turn out for the best. Don't worry."

They were the words, from the same voice, that Daniel Wilson had heard as his daughter was dying at the hospital. Oddly, though the baby was less than a year old, the voice he'd described was that of a calm, mature, sophisticated adult woman who seemed to be in charge of the situation, whatever it was.

She knocked on the door again.

Hearing voices inside No. 45, she stepped back, expecting the smiling faces of François and Asmá to pop out, welcoming her.

Instead, the door opened a foot or two, and an attractive stranger poked her head out. She looked vaguely familiar to Hannah, but Hannah had no idea why. The woman was about thirty, elegant, slender, and wearing a very pretty dark outfit consisting of black pants (cut feminine), black pumps, revealing just a hint of dark nylon stockings in the triangle between crisp cuffs and shoe straps. Her slight upper torso was clad in a dark blouse adorned with an overflow of tiny flowers that did not overwhelm the reserved theme. She had coffe-colored hair, glossy and lying in a long wave over one shoulder. Her eyes were a deep blue to match the main theme of her blouse flowers.

Hannah stammered: *Bonjour.*

The woman seemed not to see her, or totally ignored her as if Hannah weren't there.

Hannah said: "How do you do? We are here to see Asmá and François."

A young man stepped close behind the woman, also dressed in dark clothing. His suit was crisp, nicely cut, and reserved without being somber.

"What is it?" the young man said.

"I don't know," said his twin sister. "There is nobody here."

"But somebody knocked."

"It was just the wind," she said, and gently but firmly dashed the steel door shut.

Hannah was too stunned to move. Rob leaned lightly on her shoulder with one elbow. They were at a loss for words.

"There you are," said a woman's firm, pleasant take-charge voice behind them. "Welcome to the world of ghosts. You are angels here."

They turned, still stunned, and faced a beautiful golden-blonde who strode in on high, almost wobbly heels. It was the woman Hannah had bumped against in the bookstore, under the sign about ghosts.

16.   Oregon Cemetery, Paris Ghost

The beautiful woman walked toward them in the tunnel at No. 45 Rue de la Belle Ferronière in the 12th Arrondissement of Paris. She wore that same outfit as in the bookstore about two hours earlier:

Over warm pale skin, she wore a light custard-yellow summer dress flared at the knees; below that, bare legs, black high heels; her bare arms wrapped around a long glossy black leather purse with gilded snaps. Her bare hands looked pink and clean, her long fingers tipped with perfect violet-enameled nails. She wore a delicate golden Tissot wristwatch, and a slightly klunky bracelet of amber rocks on the other wrist held together by a white elastic. As she walked, her entire body seemed to balance itself with sensuous precariousness on those treacherous shoes, but she was their master and mistress. She commanded, and the shoes obeyed. "Now we are close to the fulfillment," the stranger said in her melodious, intelligent, firm voice.

"I'm sorry," Hannah said. "I am totally creeped out."

Rob stood behind her. "I'll be hiding behind Hannah."

The stranger laughed. "Let me introduce myself. My name is Claire Wilson. I am your sister. Your dad was my dad."

Hannah felt oddly rooted. "I should be fainting right now, but I feel like I just drank a pot of coffee."

Rob said behind her, wondering if he was drunk: "It's like I just drank two pitchers of beer. What in the living wazoo is going on here?"

"We need to talk," Claire or Klara said. "I think you already guessed some of the truth."

"You have a faint German accent," Hannah said.

Klara nodded. "My mother was a young woman from a village near Heidelberg."

Rob shuddered and laid both hands on Hannah's shoulders from behind, to steady himself.

"Easy, Rob," said Hannah. "I am tired of getting effed with."

"Who is effing with you?" Claire-Klara said pleasantly, without a trace of hostility, more like patience.

"Life. Fate. Daddy."

"We need to talk, kids." Pressing her glossy black purse to her side with one hand, she raised her free hand with its violet-enameled nails, and the amber bracelet, and snapped her fingers.

ഇ • ൫

Instantly, they were gone from the tunnel near Bois de Vincennes, and instead standing in a cemetery. Rob stepped up beside Hannah and exclaimed: "Oregon?"

"How is this possible?" Hannah asked. "We are in Paris."

"Not quite," Claire said. "You see, in the Paris where you were when I came to get you, you don't exist. You are ghosts, like I am in your real world."

"I'm confused," Rob said.

"I'm not surprised that we are confused," Hannah said. "I almost want to cry because this all sucks so much. I want to go home."

"You will be home soon, and everything will be better than ever," Claire said. "And so will I. Believe me, I can't wait."

"How about explaining everything?" Rob said.

"Of course. Look, there is Newport, Oregon, that small coastal city about ninety minutes west of Salem, where your parents bought a burial plot for themselves." She made a sweeping gesture with her free hand. "It is now 2018 again." Standing around the gravesite of Nancy Everol-Wilson were about thirty grieving relatives, friends, and business associates. Among them, Hannah recognized her Dad, Daniel Wilson, looking gray and bowed and every bit his age at 68. "It's 2018, and we are burying your mother. Do you see yourselves over there?" She pointed, and sure enough, there stood Rob and Hannah close together, twins to the last breath. They were dressed in dark mourning clothes, and circled by supportive cousins, uncles, and aunts.

Claire snapped her fingers again. "Let's have this past summer, 2020, the day we buried our Dad."

ഇ • ൫

The cemetery changed very little. It was drizzly, and now there were fewer people to bury Dan Wilson. He received a one-shot salute from a squad of elderly volunteer riflemen from the local American Legion hall. Over the treetops, under a mass of gray clouds, stretched the Pacific Ocean. A fresh breeze blew up from the sea, soaking the small coastal town, the hills, and the cemetery behind its wall of hedges and trees.

"This was two months ago," Hannah said.

"We were there," Rob echoed.

"Yes," Claire said, "and there I am standing near you." She pointed to a differently dressed version of herself standing among the mourners, a few rows behind Rob and Hannah, who stood together by their father's open grave as the coffin was about to be lowered in a faint drizzle.

Claire snapped her fingers again.

Part Four

Journal IV
Radiant Moon

Paris 1980-2020

17. Claire Explains Almost Everything

Now Hannah, Rob, and Claire were back in Paris, at No. 45 Rue de la Belle Ferronière. The three siblings sat at a table in the cobblestone courtyard where Hannah and Rob had first met François as he dashed a bucket of paint-slop into the central drain grating. The table might have been there or not, and Hannah couldn't recall, but it seemed appropriate. Around it were several simple wooden folding chairs that had been bleached by sunlight and many seasons of rain.

They sat together as if they had always known each other, which was not entirely untrue. But what was true—and what wasn't—in this shifting mosaic of alternative times and places, of moments and slivers of reality like a shattered mirror?

"How is it that you are alive at all?" Rob asked his older sister.

Claire was warm, imperious, and self-possessed. "It's a bit complicated. Read T. S. Eliot's *Four Quartets* to learn how all times and places rotate around each other like molecules in space, with a seamless unity, present in the same time and space. He might have worded it a bit differently, but he had the right idea. He was a man caught between two world wars, a senseless slaughter of tens of millions of souls. All for nothing. My death in Heidelberg was just one atom. T. S. Eliot's head was swimming with an ocean, a galaxy, of such atoms, men and women, children and babies who could have lived, but died in the age of Hitler, Mussolini, and Stalin as well as the lesser demagogues but no less monsters. And most of them did live, in parallel worlds with different outcomes."

"I've read Eliot," Rob said. "Loved it." He thought of Chetko. "I understand lesser monsters and all that."

"I'm still lost," Hannah said, who had had treasured a collection of Eliot's poetry since her adolescent years in Oregon. Funny, now that she thought of it, Dad had given her the book for Christmas one year, and inscribed it with a note of love for his children, plus some comment (she'd have to find it and look) about chapters of life yet to come. She shivered with chills as she recalled. She forced herself back in focus: "But Claire... I mean... what does this mean? You are alive in another dimension?"

"Sure," Claire said easily. "We'll never quite understand it, so why beat the whole thing to death?"

"So are there infinitely many worlds?" Rob asked.

"Not exactly. There is one cosmos containing infinite space and eternal time, divided into endless clouds of universes that taken in their entirety and infinity make up all possible events and outcomes. That's all we need to know. I died as an infant in your continuum, but as I died, some fate placed me in another continuum, in which I lived to grow up and become a mother and have a happy life with a husband. I came to Daddy at the saddest moment of his life, to tell him in his head everything would be okay. He wondered about that voice all of his life, until the day he died."

"And then?"

There will be more chapters in this story, he had told the twins more than once. Now all the cards seemed to be laid on the table.

Claire said: "Daddy was given a great gift, all because of Claudette Vervain's connection with Leonardo da Vinci and the *Mona Lisa*."

"I had an idea there was a connection," Hannah said.

Rob added: "Claudette Vervain was studying the old notes of Professor Benjamin Wandrous with her mentor. She and Dan were in love, but Dan left her on that bridge, so Claudette got into this hurt, self-destructive relationship with a young Belgian entrepreneur who owned a dozen laundromats across Paris. She and the Belgian died in a car crash. He was drunk as usual."

"That's right," Claire said. "Let me make all this as simple as I can. As clear as mud." She sat with her elbows on the table, as angular and graceful as a fashion model. The purse lay before her, enabling her to use both violet-tipped hands to gesticulate in pretty, rolling motions as she spoke. And speak she did: "First of all, to clear up the mystery of me. The baby who died in your world was me, as the daughter of Stana and Daddy.

"I am the daughter of Daddy and Stana's sister Hannah in my own world, where everything is just a bit different from things in your world. There was no Stanislava in my world, only my mother Hannah. My grandparents were the same—Anna Maria Bautz and Mischa Chetko, the one a cow and the other a cold-blooded war criminal with a background in the SS and the Ustasha. The difference is that they had one daughter, not two. In your world, Stana stayed in the village, while Hannah ran away after being raped by her father. Hannah never returned to that village, and ended up married to a man in Rio and having a pretty happy life except for those horrifying memories.

"So in my world, there was only my mother, Hannah, who ran away before Chetko could rape her. Bautz was out screwing about, and Chetko arrived drunk and cursing. Hannah knew what was coming, crawled out the window, and ran down the road in her nightgown under a full moon like the one that Leonardo adored so much."

"What?" Hannah asked. *Leonardo gets into this equation somehow?*

"Sorry," Claire said. "I got ahead of myself there. Backing up: my mother was given a ride by a sympathetic German salesman and his wife, who took her into Heidelberg, fed her, gave her clothes, and then took her to stay with some if their own cousins in Kirchheim, who became her foster parents. She met a U.S. soldier named Dan Wilson in my world, they married, he was my father, and there we are."

Rob asked: "But how did you end up in Dan's head the night your alter-ego died in our world?"

"That is the central motor of this story," Claire said. "You see, there are engines of fate working mysteriously that will sometimes cross different times and spaces. Daddy in your world made a tragic decision that he regretted all of his life. He wanted to remain forever with the woman he really loved, Claudette Vervain here in Paris. Instead, Stana (who did not really love him) told him she was pregnant by him, which was true, and he dutifully made the decision to be a proper father and husband with that gang in Verlorenau. He hoped against hope, and especially after I died, there was no point to it anymore. He left Germany a broken man, with nothing at all—no career, no child, no wife, and there's more; his parents back home were going through a bitter divorce, his relatives were alcoholic snakes, and so on. He returned to CONUS, and it took him ten years before he married your wonderful mother Nancy Everol, and the rest is history—in your world."

"So here we are," Hannah said, "and we are ghosts."

"You are ghosts in this world, like I am here and in your world. Think of it this way. There's your world where Dan Wilson suffers and loses his daughter (me, or my shadow).

"There is the world next to that, so to speak, where I live to be a grown woman from Dan's marriage with Hannah. My twin children are alive and well in Toronto, Canada, where we make our beautiful lives.

"There is also this third world, in which Dan Wilson stayed with Claudette Vervain in Paris. In this world, there was no marriage in Heidelberg; no baby, so I never existed nor did I die there. Stana lied in her drunken desperation, but she was never pregnant. In that world, Chetko did rape her and her sister. In the end, Hannah convinced Stana to run away with her. Neither ever returned to the village as long as Chetko was still alive. Both sisters married and had children, and Stana eventually stopped drinking and became as good a mother as Hannah.

"About Dan in that third world: he stayed in Heidelberg until his ETS in 1980. Early on, he stopped seeing Stana after he realized she had lied, that she was not pregnant. He'd always travel the four hours by train or car to visit Claudette in Paris, or she'd take the train up to see Dan in Heidelberg. The Verlorenau monsters were long and forever out of the picture. No baby, no funeral. Even his Army superiors were not the swine they were in your world.

After his separation from the Army, he moved to Paris and got a job as English-speaking manager of a department store. He married Claudette Vervain and they had two children, who are twins like you are."

A light dawned in Hannah's head. "Are those the two people who came to the door earlier?"

Claire nodded. "This is that third world. The two you saw are also twins. In this world, Claudette was not abandoned by Dan, did not take up with a drunken Belgian, and was not killed in a car crash. Dan and Claudette had two beautiful twins, like you two. Twins seem to run in the family, huh? Claudette Vervain-Wilson died in 2018, just like Nancy did in Oregon in that other continuum. And Dan Wilson died here in Paris in 2020. Those nicely dressed twins you saw were at his funeral in Père Lachaise cemetery."

"Those are beautifully parallel lives," Rob said. "Sometimes there is a mosaic piece the same, and other pieces are different. I guess it has to be that way, or the different streams of reality would be the same."

Claire said: "An expert on cosmology told me that, in her opinion, there cannot be two identical universes. There can be two that are almost the same, but each must be different by at least one molecule from all others across infinity and eternity, otherwise there will be a big annihilation implosion. *Pouf.*" She made a *pouf*-motion with her fists, knocking them together and then making them fly apart.

Hannah said: "The part I don't get is why all this is happening? Why were you brought from your continuum to talk to Daddy in his head? Why are we going through all this?

"Because," Claire said, "as I said, there are forces at work, maybe gods or angels or who knows what. Our Dad was needed for an important mission that required him to marry Claudette Vervain and stand by her, have children, help support a household here, while Claudette and her professor uncovered the final secret of Leonardo da Vinci."

"And what is that?" Rob asked.

"Slow down a moment longer," Claire said. "In the Dan plus Claudette world, Claudette uncovered the great secret of Leonardo's *Mona Lisa*. In your world, that secret was lost when Dan abandoned her, she ran off with the Belgian, and they died in a car crash. So the forces that run the show felt an imperative need to have that secret also revealed in your world. And they had to use a roundabout method to avoid contradictions. Because once you introduce contradictions, there could be rippling domino effects across an unknown number of parallel worlds." Claire took a breath. "I am almost done here. I can't wait for my life to be simple again." She sighed deeply. "I'll miss you two."

"So you have a husband and children in Toronto?" Hannah asked.

Claire nodded. "Everything I do here is in extra time. I don't lose anything with my own family. It's like all this is happening while I am in bed sleeping with Richard. My husband. Let's not even go there. Does not concern you nor does it matter in this continuum. And my two children are about to begin middle school in Toronto, where we live. You know what? When we are done here, you will forget all this ever happened. I will also forget. We'll never know that we knew each other. But the difference will be that your world will learn the secret of Leonardo, even though nothing else changes. Well, not quite."

"What do you mean?"

"Dan Wilson was given a promise. And so was Claudette. It was as much because of their individual sufferings, as it was about rewarding Leonardo da Vinci by exposing his grand secret in yet another world—yours."

"When they died, the promise was a fabulous gift: that at their deaths in your world, they would each return to the moment when they split up, when Dan abandoned her on that bridge in Paris. That is how that third world came into being, at the moment when Dan and Claudette turn around and run toward each other on the Passerelle des Arts in front of the Louvre, rather than away from each other. They run toward each other with open arms, hug and dance about with laughter and tears, and are inseparable."

"The Bridge of Regret," Rob said. "He mentions it in his journals."

"The Pont des Arts," Claire said. "A *passerelle* or foot-bridge over the Seine.'"

"So in front of the Louvre is where they said goodbye," Rob said.

Claire nodded. "In tears, yes, both of them. At that moment, your world lost a wonderful secret about Leonardo's creation, the most famous painting in the history of the world. With that enigmatic smile."

"What is she smiling about?" Hannah asked rather frivolously.

"You'll find out shortly."

"Are we done here?" Rob asked.

"Almost. It remains now for you two to fulfill one last little item. But first, there is a wonderful thing you need to know."

"I'm all ears," Rob said.

"Me too," Hannah said.

"You found the Journals of Daniel Wilson. Numbers I, II, and III."

Hannah's turn to snap her fingers, sitting there in the courtyard. "I'm going to guess that there is a fourth one. Journal IV."

"Exactly," Claire said. "*Touché.*"

"She is the smart one sometimes," Rob admitted about his twin sister.

Hannah slapped him lightly on the hand. "I'm just speaking out loud for both of us."

"Do we get to read that journal?" Rob asked.

"Not exactly," Claire said. "You see, Journal IV not a written one but a living one. Much like the Journal I that François gave you, Journal IV is a big fat beautiful, happy scrapbook. It is the living record of when the two lovers were reborn at that bridge and had a second shot at life. Claudette, who died in a car crash, instead got a new life in a parallel world. So did Dan, all because he did not abandon her. He was finished with his ETS soon enough, and came to Paris to make a new life with her." She added: "Fate ordained that there would be an extra time and space, a new parallel world, in which Dan died in Oregon at 72, and came back here as a young soldier in his twenties, where he made the decision, on the bridge, at that moment back in 1977, not to leave Claudette, but to as her to marry him. And she said yes, gladly, hugging him and crying with him. The wonder of it was that she'd live to solve the mystery of Leonardo, and they would have wonderful lives with those two nice twin children you saw, now grown up after Dan and Claudette have died."

Rob said softly: "No Chetko, no village of the damned."

As Claire spoke, the door at No. 45 opened, and those same elegant twins emerged, dressed in dark clothing. "They are going to a special ceremony at the Louvre," Claire explained. "It's a very big day, honoring their mother Claudette and father Daniel, who have the honor of lying buried together in Père Lachaise Cemetery in the Twentieth Arrondissement."

Hannah said: "Isn't that only for famous people?"

"Precisely," Claire said. "Their grave of honor is not far from that of Jim Morrison, and a lot of other famous people, including Peter Abelard of medieval times, Honoré de Balzac the author, actress Sarah Bernhardt, Jean de Brunhoff who gave us Babar the Elephant, glass designer René Lalique, singer Édith Piaf, English author Oscar Wilde, and a long list of other greats."

Hannah felt overwhelmed. "Claudette then... she really did accomplish something wonderful."

"Uncovering the secret of the *Mona Lisa*'s smile," Rob seconded.

Claire nodded yes, then nodded toward the young couple getting into a taxi. Also coming out of the house were several nicely dressed little children, and another man and woman. "The twins in this world, Danielle named after Dan Wilson, and Claude named after his mother, and their spouses, and children."

"Nice families," Rob said.

"Very nice," Claire agreed. "We have all been lucky, except the victims of Chetko and the cow, emblematic of much of humankind on a bad day."

"In a bad universe," Rob said.

"It's not funny," Hannah said. "I hope those lost souls find peace."

Claire shrugged lightly. She rose. *Time to go.*

"Time to step outside of the living Journal IV of Dan Wilson," Hannah said. "We return to our lives in parallel separate worlds. Time to say goodbye."

"So right," Claire agreed. "I am finished here. Goodbye, brother and sister." She hugged each of them and then turned and walked out of the tunnel, vanishing before their eyes.

ℬ • ℭ

"Wow," said Rob.

"You can say that again."

"Wow," said Rob again in the same tone.

Hannah picked up the paper sack of notes from Wandrous in the 1930s, and Claudette in the 1980s. They started to walk in the direction where the car with Dan and Claudette's children had driven, which was also the direction in which Claire had just forever disappeared.

"Hey, you guys!" a man's voice called out behind them.

Rob and Hannah turned, and there were François and Asmá.

"What are you doing?" Asmá asked brightly. She wore her girl-dress, a simple thing in dark red that came to just above her knees, and flew about freely as she walked. Her light-coffee legs were bare and beautiful, as were her lively swinging arms and her long, delicate fingers tipped with red lacquer. Her glossy pageboy bobbed this way and that. Her dark eyes flashed. Red lipstick shaped a smile, revealing perfect white teeth.

François was his usual tall, reserved, but friendly self as he hovered near Asmá. "We tried calling you," he said rather lamely.

"We got tied up," Hannah said. She held up the papers. "Look what we have."

"Did you read the Journal I?" Asmá asked.

At that moment, Rob's cell phone rang. "It's Elise," he said. "She and Yves are pacing up and down frantically looking for us by the Shakespeare & Company Bookstore."

"Tell them we'll be on our way shortly," Hannah said. To Asmá and François she said: "We need to shmooze."

Asmá and François looked at each other, then at Hannah, and shrugged. "What is shmooze?"

"Be friends," Rob said.

Asmá and François nodded happily. François said: "I am your relative somehow. A cousin, or a nephew, I'm not sure which."

As the taxi arrived a moment later, and Rob opened the door for her, Hannah said to their new family: "This weekend, dinner in the Quartier Latin? Drinks?"

"You're on," François and Asmá cried happily, waving.

"Wow," Rob said in the back seat, as the taxi took him and Hannah back toward the bookstore to retrieve Elise and Yves.

"You already said that twice," Hannah teased.

He shook his head. "I'll say it again." And he did.

Wow.

18. *Mona Lisa*: Radiant Moon

A few days later, Rob and Hannah Wilson entered the Louvre grounds, accompanied by Elise and Yves. They were on their way to the most important appointment of all—with Madame Tournesol, the museum's executive director.

Hannah and Yves (who was beaming because he had just received a major contract with a recording studio) stayed close together.

Rob held Elise by one arm, and with his other hand carried a briefcase containing the paper sack with the research done by Wandrous in this time continuum in the 1930s, and examined by the late Claudette Vervain before she died tragically in a car crash in 1982. That car crash happened in this world, which Hannah thought of as the first of the parallel worlds she knew, out of infinitely many universes in which all outcomes did occur.

Nothing—well, almost nothing—would change in this first parallel world. Hannah's memory was already hazy, but she remembered (still, just for now) that there was a third parallel world in which Dan returned to Paris and married Claudette.

Inbetween was a second parallel world containing Claire, who had been the baby not of Stana but of Hannah. There was no Stanislava in that second world, only Hannah who had escaped the horror of that village and led a beautiful life far away with a husband in Berlin. Claire, in turn, married a Canadian and moved to Toronto, where she and Richard raised two—of course—fraternal twins, a boy and girl.

Hannah and Rob were born in the first world, of Dan's nightmare in Heidelberg and his regret about that bridge in Paris, the world in which the baby did die (a tiny angel now in eternity, forever bouncing and laughing on the knees of her laughing and crying young parents in that hospital room). This was the world in which the discoveries of Wandrous in the 1930s and Claudette in the 1980s, lost in that deadly car crash, had been rediscovered by Hannah and Rob working with a lot of sympathetic, wonderful people including Mme Tournesol and Monsieur Bondie and their unnamed research assistants (or angels) along with ghosts in the bookstore in the Rue de la Bûcherie. This was the world in which Claire, and angel or ghost from the next world over, accomplished her mission of helping in that rediscovery, and unveiling the secret of Leonardo. The discovery would leak across into the world of Hannah and Rob.

The third parallel world was that in which Dan broke off with Stana, fnished his second enlistment to its ETS in Heidelberg, and then returned to Paris to marry the real love of his life, Claudette. It was the world in which Dan and Claudette each got a chance to return to that moment on the Passerelle or footbridge before the Louvre, and do things differently. In this third world, Claudette would marry Dan and have the two well-dressed twins Hannah had seen in the tunnel in the Twelfth Arrondissement. And, in that alternate reality, Claudette would find the lost papers of Professor Wandrous, and reveal to the world the forgotten secret of Leonardo's devotion to a portrait of Lisa Gherardini of Florence while working in France near the end of his life in the early 1500s.

With the help of Claire from that second reality, Dan would receive a message of hope and continuity at the saddest moment of his life, and a promise (because some higher power valued the magic of Leonardo so much) to give Dan and Claudette a restart on their lives. The Mona Lisa's secret would be revealed in that world, and leaked into the first world of Hannah and Rob as well.

These things would not be explained to Madame Tournesol—only the actual secret of the Mona Lisa. And wasn't that enough?

ဢ • ಚ

A museum guide in uniform blazer, looking very official, escorted them to the office of Madame Tournesol, who had cleared an hour on her calendar for the important news that the *Americains* and their European friends were bringing to her. The telephone call from Mademoiselle Hannah Wilson had been sufficient to tell Madame Tournesol that this was a very important bit of information.

The guide ushered Hannah and Rob in to Madame Tournesol's office and closed the big, quiet door behind them. Mme Tournesol rose and shook their hands. She bade them to take seats. "I am all excited," she said. "I cannot wait until you tell me what you have learned."

Rob spread the papers on the desk before Mme Tournesol and sat down beside his sister.

Hannah took the lead in talking. "You know that the *Mona Lisa* is the most famous painting in the world, and her smile is one of the great secrets in art history. We are convinced that Professor Wandrous was onto it, and that Mademoiselle Claudette Vervain rediscovered it."

"So we are not taking any credit," Rob said humbly and honestly. "We want Wandrous and Vervain to get the full credit for this discovery."

Mme Tournesol shrugged. *Easy enough. Go on...*

By turns, Hannah and Rob explained what they had learned from hours of reading and studying the notes, with the help of Yves as translator. Elise and Yves sitting on the outside while the twins sat between them, listened with great interest and pride. Mme Tournesol held her questions until the end, and then was too flabberghasted to have any questions. Here is the story that Rob and Hannah told from the notes of Claudette Vervain (attached as the final chapter), whose sources included the lost researches of Professor Benjamin Wandrous from the 1930s (who vanished during the German occupation, and is known to have been deported via Drancy to Auschwitz, where he was murdered along with so many other innocents).

As Hannah and Rob explained:

ॐ • ☙

The image of the *Mona Lisa* is a representation of both an adorable wife in a wealthy Florence household around 1500, as well as Leonardo da Vinci's spiritual exploration of themes relating to life, mortality, and the feminine divine.

Mona Lisa is Leonardo's portrait of a smiling Woman in the Moon, as our studies strongly suggest. As our notes show, the painting is a superimposed, private reproduction of his earlier portrait of Lisa Gherardini and of the moon (Greek Selene or Mene; Latin Luna).

Nobody paid him to pursue this work. It was a private, personal passion of this Renaissance man, applying the same courageous and fresh ideas to his lunar-feminine study as he did with all other matters.

We will let his handiwork speak for itself. We have appended the notes and drawings of Professor Wandrous and Candidate Vervain in the following chapters.

We can only hope to briefly present a summary of their case before you today, Madame Tournesol.

ॐ • ☙

Our endeavor is to present some historical context in which this wonder took place—since the painting has become the most famous in history, and her smile one of the great mysteries of the past half-millennium.

From his notebooks, we know that Leonardo believed the moon harbored landscapes much as did the earth he knew, primarily of peninsular Italy. The gardens behind the Mona Lisa could be a typical Renaissance Italian palace garden or manorial hunting forest. However, from our study of the painting, we propose that he has painted his concept of a lunar landscape, self-illumined in a sort of metaphoric mirror image, by the moon (*Mond, Luna, Mene, Mona,*) herself.

That is the great secret of the *Mona Lisa*. Her name is ambiguous. The German word for moon is Mond, and the name Lisa can easily be conflated with the same Indo-European root that gives us the German word *Licht* or the English *Light*, as in Latin *lux*. Taking aside various ambitious and not implausible translations ('mona' or 'monna' as aunt in Italian, and so forth) we may also follow Professor Wandrous' and Claudette Vervain's theory to their conclusion that the title of the painting really means **Radiant Moon**.

ಬಿ • ಅ

When Mme Tournesol heard all this, she sat in stunned silence for a minute or two. Finally, she pointed to the documents. "Thank you ever so much. Can I make copies for our archives here in the Louvre?"

"Of course," Hannah said, pushing the packet of documents forward.

Already, her memories were becoming clouded, as the golden-haired (who was that again?) woman had predicted. *Claire de lune, light of the moon, Mona Lisa...*

As a final touch, while Rob and Hannah said goodbye to Mme Tournesol, and prepared to leave with their loved ones—Elise and Yves—to start their lives and families in earnest, nobody noticed one tiny detail that became forever part of the historical record—another little mystery that nobody would ever have the means to figure out, should the question even be asked.

Credit for the discovery was to be forever given, in the fine print of an obscure footnote reference, to two persons: Professor Benjamin Wandrous, and to a young (long deceased) graduate student whose name was given as Madame Claudette Vervain-Wilson. The form of address (madame) in French normally signals a married woman. It is a slight fib, given that the abandoned lover of Daniel Wilson at the Bridge of Regret never married in her short life, in that same reality in which Dan eventually married Nancy and begat Hannah and Rob. Nobody but Hannah and Rob would ever notice, and they would soon forget as they would soon also not recall the angel Claire from a parallel reality. As to lost baby Klara, those who cross over such bridges become angels and live forever. Also living forever are the eternal smile of *Mona Lisa*, and the melody of *Clair de Lune*.

Appendices: From Notes of Claudette Vervain &al.

Appendix 1: Notes of Candidate Mme. Claudette Vervain-Wilson
Master's Thesis Paris 1950-1981 (At Her Untimely Death)
Based on Mixed Notes of Prof. Benjamin Wandrous (1892-1940)
Before His Untimely Death at Auschwitz

Appendix 2: Sketches by Prof. Benjamin Wandrous (1892-1940)
Relating Mona Lisa and the Moon

ଏ ● ଓ

19.　Appendix 1: Leonardo—Studies by Claudette Vervain

ॐ ● ☙

Introduction

The Louvre painting of the *Mona Lisa* is a representation of both an adorable wife in a wealthy Florence household around 1503, as well as Leonardo da Vinci's spiritual exploration of themes relating to life, mortality, and the feminine divine.

Our studies suggest that the *Mona Lisa* is Leonardo's composite of a smiling Woman in the Moon. As our notes show, the painting is a superimposed, private reproduction of his earlier portrait of Lisa Gherardini (completed, delivered, and lost to time) and of the moon (Greek Selene or Mene; Latin Luna).

Nobody paid him to pursue this work after he fulfilled his contract and delivered to Francesco del Giocondo a first version. The Louvre version was a private, personal passion of this Renaissance man, applying the same courageous and fresh ideas to his lunar-feminine study as he did with all other matters.

The notes of Professor Wandrous and Claudette Vervain bring to us a plausible understanding of the theology, the chemistry, the passion. Like Newton two centuries later, Leonardo can well be called the world's last great magician, and its first great scientist.

We will let his handiwork speak for itself. Our endeavor is to present some historical context in which this wonder took place—since the painting has become the most famous in history, and her smile one of the great mysteries of the past half-millennium.

Courage During Inquisition

As a first matter of context, consider Leonardo's courage. He was a fierce rational investigator who gained license from the medical authorities in Florence and Milan to dissect corpses, in order to study the mechanical aspects of the musculature underlying facial expressions as well as moving limbs. Leonardo lived in an age of Inquisition, when people could still be burned alive for even the faintest suggestion of heresy.

Just consider the living incineration of the monk Giordano Bruno in a public square of Rome, in 1600, almost a century after Leonardo painted his Mona Lisa. As late as the 1630s, the same Church that had outpaced the world with its cutting edge Jesuit calendar, the Gregorian, in the 1580s, still clung to an earth-centered universe and came close to consigning Galileo Galilei to a similar fate as Giordano Bruno's, although Galileo managed to get away with house arrest and silencing for the rest of his earthly life.

In those same perilously dark ages, many courageous or crazy souls pursued the study of dangerous arts like alchemy or astrology, which had their origins in Classical antiquity. You had one foot in the 'pagan' world, and the other foot in the European-Medieval Christian world. Lean too hard the wrong way, and you might be tortured and burned as a heretic. Lean the other way, and you might be a hero at the courts of popes and kings.

Just think that Sir Isaac Newton (1642-c1724), the great English polymath, made his living casting horoscopes and working alchemies for the superstitious dukes and bishops of England while, at night, he secretly pursued risky studies in the sciences—like optics and astronomy—and became co-inventor of the orbital calculus with Kepler. Newton has been called both 'the last great magician' and 'the first great scientist.' Newton, it will suffice to say, died two centuries after Leonardo, so we can imagine Leonardo's great caution in an age when the smoke of burning heretics was ever a faint warning whiff in the air.

It was an age of Rebirth (Renaissance) maturing into the modern age. The Church was both an ancient and a medieval ship sailing into a sea of modern Enlightenment and Humanism. We take no sides in these matters, because the Europe through which we journey today is a field of ruined churches, castles, and palaces left by rampaging mobs serving the cynical overlords of new or old dogmatic systems. The Reformation had not yet quite occurred, though it hung in the atmosphere with an explosive potential energy; and Luther posted his Ninety-Five Thesis on the church door at Wittemburg in 1517, just two years before Leonardo's death.

Like other free thinkers of his age dabbling in alchemy, astrology, and Classical 'pagan' mythologies, Leonardo had to be extremely careful not to run afoul of the theological police.

Personalities: Lisa

Lisa Gherardini was born on June 15th, 1479 into a well-to-do household in downtown Florence, at a time when Florence was one of the great city-states in Italy and, indeed, of the world.

When Leonardo first painted her portrait, Lisa was about 25 years old, the mother of five children of whom one had already died in infancy. Lisa was the third wife of Florence merchant Francesco del Gioconda of old and wealthy family. The original painting, which we can be sure was delivered to Francesco del Giocondo, was a joyful celebration of Lisa's survival through childbirth into motherhood, giving him four children. A fifth child, a baby girl, died in infancy in 1499. None of this was unusual for that age, but we know from contemporary letters and other documents that survivors grieved terribly, as they would in our time.

Far worse happened during the time that Leonardo was painting and re-painting Lisa's image in Chambord. A second child of the Jocondi died at 18, their beautiful Beatrice who had become a nun. The melancholy of her joys and tragedies is reflected behind the playful, tolerant humor in her eyes, not to mention the sweetness of her motherly smile. Leonardo captured this in all of his genius and empathy. We do not know what became of the painting delivered to Giocondo by Leonardo around 1503, so we don't know precisely what its title might have been, if any. Maybe Francesco simply adored her as 'my love.' We will never know. Whatever the truth, Lisa lives forever in her portrait, with its cosmic secret soon to be revealed, the ultimate tribute of Leonardo to the divine in all of us.

Lisa Gherardini's married name (del Giocondo) offered a facile play on words, ostensibly meaning 'the smiling one.' She was married to the wealthy Francesco del Giocondo. This wealthy silk merchant of Florence had much to celebrate with her. He had been married twice before, and each of those young women met a fate common to so many women before the modern age of hygiene and better medical understanding: dying in childbirth. So the commission to have Lisa's portrait painted by a renowned artist (Leonardo) was a moment of joy and celebration. One could speculate that her mysterious smile might simply stem from being happy to be alive, but Professor Wandrous' papers show he uncovered a rather different (and not mutually exclusive) reason.

ༀ • ༀ

Her enigmatic smile has become notorious around the world for centuries. Why is she smiling, and what did Leonardo want to achieve?

The immediate reason for her smile has already been mentioned. Lisa was the third wife of wealthy merchant Francesco del Giocondo, who was much older than Lisa. Francesco's previous two young wives had died tragically in childbirth, as was very common in that age. So, to make short of the matter, her sweet, slightly pained smile is that of a survivor. Her husband had ample reason to commission such a portrait. He and his family are celebrating all at once Lisa's survival in bearing five children, his joy at being a father so many times, and their happiness together. Of the five children, an infant daughter died in 1499, which contributes a touch of tender melancholy to the character of Lisa, as captured by Leonardo in her portrait. More than anything, that shadow of sadness can be detected around her eyes.

Leonardo exquisitely captured her feminine nature as an attractive young women, and also as a mother both joyous and suffering. A thousand years of portraying the suffering Virgin Mary prepared him for this step outside the accepted bounds into the Classical world. Like other intellectuals of his time, he had to keep secret his inner motives, often veiling them behind conventions and false fronts. To capture the spirit of the suffering mother (convention: Mater Dolorosa, Grieving Mother), we need only consider Michelangelo's Pietà of 1498 or 99 (same year that Lisa lost her baby daughter) or we can look into the eyes and facial expressions of many surviving Eastern icons showing Mary as Theotokos (God-Bearer).

Personalities: Leonardo

Leonardo exercised his powers of observation by doing what came best to him: drawing and painting objects to visualize their scientific (and, we think, spiritual) context. We would call it his way of thinking out loud. That is his intellectual, artistic side. On the other hand, he was a sensitive, caring man; enigmatic, but warm and passionate.

As a native of Florence, born and living not far from Lisa's familes (both the Gherardini and the Giocondi), had to have been acutely and humanly aware of the woman sitting so sweetly, humorously, and filled with humanity before him for hours as he sketched her and then painted her. She was a wife, a mother, and a woman. Neither the painting man nor the sitting woman could have imagined that he would become world-famous for centuries to come, and she would become the most famous woman in history. Both would become household names, and what happened in that space enclosing them both would be nothing short of magic. Her personality still sparkles in our century, and will enchant viewers for ages to come.

Leonardo moved to France in his final years and worked at the Chateau de Chambord in the Loire Valley of France, not very far from Paris and King François I, in the decade before Leonardo's death at 67 in 1519. As always, he was pursuing courageous and original investigations.

ಬಿ • ಛ

Leonardo da Vinci was a mysterious figure in his own right. He was a Renaissance genius, dabbling in technology and sciences, in philosophy and art. He made many more sketches, all very famous, than the handful of great paintings—but his paintings were rated in a category of genius and brilliance all their own.

Leonardo da Vinci was born in humbler circumstances on a farm in the village of Vinci outside Florence, on April 15, 1452, making him about 27 years older than Lisa.

Leonardo worked in Florence and Milan for much of his productive early life, serving various Renaissance clients, and finally moved to Rome where his patron was Pope Pius X. He traveled with the pope to Bologna to meet King François I of France, who at that time was perhaps the strongest political player in both Francia and the Italian states. In his final years (1513-1519),

Leonardo moved into François' beautiful Loire Valley estate Château d'Amboise, in a picturesque region famous for its gardens and grapevines.

When he died in 1519, Leonardo left an estate behind that included the *Mona Lisa*, as most people in the modern world refer to La Gioconda (Italian) or La Joconde (French).

Driving Passion: Leonardo as Mystic

What was that driving passion that kept Leonardo coming back time and again to the highly nuanced painting of this sweet but ordinary woman— pretty, delicate, characterful, but not a stunning beauty like the most glamorous face of her era, Simonetta Cattaneo Vespucci (1453-1476) who died tragically at 22. Leonardo, born in April 1452, was just months older than Simonetta, and thus her contemporary, moving in the atmosphere and ambience of Simonetta's renowned grace and beauty. Simonetta was likely the subject of Andrea Boticelli's famous painting that hangs in the Städler Museum, Frankfurt am Main, in Germany; and maybe Boticelli's paintings— *Birth of Venus* out of sea foam, based on an ancient myth; and his famous *Primavera*, or Spring, in which Simonetta is reputed to be one of the three Muses, or maybe she modeled all three. In any case, the Smiling One is a plainer beauty, but no less dramatic. By 1506, let's say, Lisa Gherardini would have been about thirty years old. Something kept driving Leonardo to this particular painting.

A clue about his reticent, secretive life comes from Florence in 1476, when Leonardo, along with at least three wealthy young men, was arrested by the authorities in Florence on accusations of sodomy. The investigation was quashed, probably because the wealthy parents paid everyone off to kill the story. It lingers like a taint around Leonardo's life, and is particularly interesting because he never married. He shows passionate feelings for beauty in both male and female figures, while at the same time never shying away from sketching grotesque faces (because of his scientific studies of musculature in both living subjects and in cadavers). The world will probably never know what the precise (or blurry, sfumato) nature of Leonardo's gender identity may have been.

Leonardo had a tendency to tackle too many projects all at once, performing brilliantly at everything he touched. The major rub was that he often did not finish projects. He was, in effect, all over the map as they say. His gender orientation is not entirely clear. His relationships with women remain a bit of a cipher, particularly since he never married, and there is no record of a single woman in whatever love life he may or may not have had. And yet, still, he had a touch for beauty—and he brings out the best in Lisa Gherardini, to the extent that she is arguably the most famous face in history.

And unlike so many of his projects, he keeps coming back to this one for years, without a patron for the work, and at no pay.

Now remember that he was a deep thinker. Among this theories was that the moon has an atmosphere, and presumably landscapes like we see on Earth. His notebooks comment on the earth-like terrain of the moon.

Next point: He is also a major figure at the tail end of the European Renaissance. The word renaissance is French and means rebirth. The rebirth in question was of Classical texts, primarily in Hellenic or Greek. For a thousand years, Christian theology had been driven by a rather limited understanding from Latin translations surviving the collapse of the Classical or ancient world, specifically the Roman empire, which we may consider to be the last gasp of Hellenism. Roman civilization, and the Christian infrastructure that survived it into modern times, was a Hellenistic civilization based on ancient Greek philosophy and social theory. Medieval scholars like Francis Bacon, Thomas Aquinas, and the like based their works on surviving texts from Plotinus, Augustine, Boethius, and a handful of other geniuses of Late Antiquity. After 1300, the West was flooded with manuscripts from the collapsing Byzantine and Arabic empires.

Baghdad was sacked by the Mongols in 1248, causing hundreds of renowned scholars to flee to the remaining free Arab and Berber provinces in Iberia or Spain. This opened the door for ancient manuscripts that had been long lost, and new translations, including those in the Bible. In fact, during Leonardo's lifetime, Pope Sixtus V commissioned a rebuilding of the Capella Magna, the Great Chapel of the popes in Rome, which thereafter was known as the Sistine Chapel. Pope Sixtus put many famous artists to work painting the walls and ceiling, surprisingly not with Christian thematics for the most part, but blending ancient Jewish and Hellenistic mythologies and traditions to somehow try and reconcile a thousand years of Christian theology based at centers like Rome and Constantinople with more ancient writings from the age of Christ and Octavian (Augustus).

The Sistine Chapel thus is a kind of theological attack (or defense) submarine, designed to stabilize and reconcile a Christian theology shaken by the Renaissance. Against that backdrop, Leonardo (who was not involved with the Sistine Chapel, but knew many of the artists who were) had to have been acutely aware of ancient mythologies.

He would also have been sensitive to the personal reasons why the Florentine silk merchant del Giocondo wanted to celebrate his sweet wife in *painture*. Lisa Gherardini was a survivor, a grievously wounded but smiling victor over the forces of death that killed so many women and children, like young Simonetta Vespucci, and two of Lisa's own children. Lisa finished her years withdrawn to a cloister of nuns.

Now comes the revelation of Benjamin Wandrous, as revealed to the world through the notes of Claudette Vervain for her Master's thesis. Namely, Leonardo was growing older. He was conscious of his mortality, and he captured the smile of the survivor in Lisa Gherardini's facial expression.

As a scientist, however, he took this a step further. How would one translate that brief, short-lived triumph of life over death, that uniquely female and feminine power to carry life and give birth, into something permanent? Where would one look? Where did Leonardo look? Deep inside, at his own relationships with the feminine.

Leonardo, who was a modern man living in a reborn Classical age, combined his scientific theories with newly in vogue Classical subjects, and looked up at the moon.

Traditionally, the masculine had been associated with sky gods like the thundering Jupiter of Rome (*deus pater*) or Zeus of Athens (actually *theos pater)*. The feminine in nature was associated more than anything else with the moon goddesses in cultures where the moon is female. That excludes Japanese and Germanic models (*der Mond* or the moon in German is masculine, whereas die Sonne or the sun is masculine); and in Mesopotamia, the moon god is masculine, associated with the bull; but these are the exceptions. From very ancient times we have young, feral virginal deities like the Achaean Helen, Greek Artemis, or Roman Diana all of whom are warriors. In fact, in later Roman mythology, Diana gives rise to a male persona when an added month is needed for the archaic ten-month calendar, and that becomes Ianus (hence January), where Diana or Iana morphs genders into Ianus (who lives on in modern times as a grim reaper Saturn holding a harrowing sicle over one arm, and the new year's baby in his other arm, sometimes along with a rather ominous hourglass.

So it appears that Leonardo, whose feminine side was always ambivalent, took the survivor smile of Lisa Gherardini, and sought a spiritual immortality of sorts in a universal phenomenon that has informed human mythology and consciousness since the Old Stone Age. Namely, hers becomes the face in the moon.

Photographic and photonegative studies by Wandrous, as well as overlays and sketches, show a strong resemblance between features on the painting's round head and face with features of a full moon.

Not only that, but the seeming Italian pastoral background may then be taken as reflecting (no pun intended) Leonardo's theory that the moon had an atmosphere and features including forests and lakes, much like the Earth.

That is the great secret of the *Mona Lisa*. Her name is ambiguous. The German word for moon in Mond, and the name Lisa can easily be conflated with the same Indo-European root that gives us the German word *Licht* or the English *Light*, as in Latin *lux*. Taking aside various ambitious and not implausible translations ('mona' or 'monna' as aunt in Italian, and so forth) we may also follow Professor Wandrous' and Claudette Vervain's theory to its conclusion that the title of the painting really suggests Radiant Moon.

꒰ • ꒱

Leonardo was male, so we begin with his gender orientation, which has confused scholars for half a millennium. He is known to have been a super-talented, brilliant, complex, loving, reclusive and enigmatic man. He never married, and he had one brush with gender dysfamia or dysphoria early in his life (about age 24) when he and some some aristocratic friends were arrested by Florentine authorities responding to secret accusations vaguely labeled as sodomy, which is usually taken to mean sexual activity with same gender. Evidently, wealthy relatives must have paid to have any taint quashed, and maybe it wasn't as uncommon as one might think, so nothing else ever rose to that level of scandal again. That incident, and other circumstantial evidence, lead us to conclude he possessed an ambivalent and superambient gender orientation that remains undefinable; and it informs all of his brilliant artistic works.

The sitter in the painting is female, so the angle of pursuit becomes the question of Leonardo's relationships with women. There are many accompanying notes. To contain them the margin of this treatise is too small, so this is a brief summary of highlights.

The sitter is a young Florentine housewife, Lisa Gherardini. She is in her early twenties at the time of sitting, and we believe the original commission for her portrait must have been fulfilled. We know this only circumstantially, from a lack of legal action or other outcry in case Leonardo had not fulfilled his contract.

Painting's Title

What about the painting's title? The names by which she is most commonly known (*Mona Lisa*, *Gioconda*) were attributed later. In fact, it originated with painter and art historian Giorgio Vasari (1511-1574) in a biography of Leonardo that Vasari published in 1550.

We can only venture a brief but revealing sketch of the linguistic (etymological) and cultural issues. We must remind ourselves that the primary evidence is visual (the painting itself), while the title is more ephemeral.

We cautiously propose that whatever title Leonardo may have had in mind (resembling those commonly used today, like *Mona Lisa*) would best be taken as a double entendre. That is, we should take literally the historical fact that the sitter's name was Lisa, and yet we may read into that a second layer of meaning related to *lux*, light (see notes following). In the final analysis, the linguistic analysis of the title quickly leads into many fragmented directions,

and we remain best positioned at the ambivalent juncture of—on one side—
Mona Lisa (Madame Lisa) and—on the other side—the concept here
developed, euphoniously rendered as **Radiant Moon**.

Somewhere, buried in all this, is a possible but unlikely triple entendre,
in that the most important symbol of French royalty has been the lily, or *fleur-
de-lis* (literally, "lily flower"), which would have had special significance to
Leonardo's patron, King François I of France.

We may accept the well-documented etymologies of Mona, meaning
essentially Madame or Aunt (two different meanings), and yet we see the
shadow of certain planetary terms behind it expressed via metaphor (*Mene* or
Mond as moon; Mondo or Monde as world). Leonardo, like many free
thinkers and rational skeptics of his age, would have been well-served by the
shielding ambiguity, an intended self-protection in an age of Inquisition that
still burned people alive for suspected heresies.

Note that there is also an Italian word *zia* for aunt, comparable to Spanish
tia, but again that is in virtual certainty a jejeune direction to take, like the
fleur-de-lis. If anything, one treads across a minefield of 'false friends'
(deceptive etymologies) by getting too far afield with these exercises.

ꝏ • ꞔꞡ

The title Leonardo may have had in mind for his private or second
painting was probably as ambiguous as the image itself. We suggest that the
later-given title *Mona Lisa* may just as well reflect some slippery
etymological fish to catch, referring not to Lisa Gherardini so much as to her
metaphorical representation of the Classical feminine moon (Mene, Luna,
Selene).

Comparing contemporary works, we find it was apparently uncommon to
give fanciful titles to portraits, no matter how illustrious the patron or how
beautiful the sitter. From various later sources came titles like *Mona Lisa* (or
Monna Lisa, which might mean something like Aunt Lisa, an unlikely title for
her husband to order). Another common name is *La Gioconda* or *La Joconde*,
the Smiling One, a pun on her married name (del Giocondo).

Other, contemporary paintings have come down to us without standard
titles, perhaps a convention of the age. A notable example is the portraiture of
Simonetta Vespucci (1453-1476), who died tragically young like many
women of her time, at around age 22, probably in childbirth. Simonetta, the
likely sitter for Sandro Boccaccio's masterpieces (*Birth of Venus, Primavera*,
etc.) was considered the most beautiful woman in all of northern Italy. By
coincidence, she was born a year before Leonardo, and died when he was
about 23 years old. They might have met, who knows? She was painted by
many late Renaissance painters. Her paintings on classical themes have

predicable titles, but her more personal portraits do not seem to have titles other than later attributions.

So in the end, we may attribute an underlying title (hidden from the Inquisition under layers of metaphor, obscurity, and *sfumato*) that picks up on ambient Indo-European names from both the Germanic and Romance sides (Leonardo's milieu; the Indo-European language family is the world's largest, encompassing hundreds of languages and patoix that now span the globe).

In modern German, be way of exception, the word for moon (although masculine) is *der Mond*, which echoes rather closely the word Mona (not the Italian word *monna* for aunt).

The the Italian *mona* (for aunt or mistress) may be a contraction of the words *ma donna* (my mistress, understandable in various constructions like the French *monsieur*, from *mon sieur*, my lord and *madame, ma dame*, my lady). Taking madonna further back linguistically, one finds *mea domina* or *mea domna* (my lady in Latin Vulgate; *domina mea* in ancient Latin). In that sense, the best rendering of *Mona* would be Madame, or Signora (another Latin derivation, from *senior*, elder in the comparative form; *senex*, old man as an adjective or noun, as in *Senatus*, Senate). It should not strike the modern ear as entirely odd if the intention is Madame Lisa; because until relatively modern times, European Medieval and Renaissance-era persons did not usually bear a family name except in the case of landed gentry, and in time the occupations of commoners (e.g., smith, cooper, scribner, baker, tanner); or by use of a suffix (*-son, -sdottir, -ov* or *-ova*) the creation of a family name from an ancestral given name.

Classical lunar deities, all female, included the Greek Selene and the Roman Luna. However, another Greek or Hellenic name for Selene was Mene; how close to Mona is that?

Finally, the word Lisa is the sitter's given name. Consider, however, in Leonardo's clever mind, how similar might those words be to terms for 'light' or 'radiant.' The Latin word for light is *lux*, and a Roman goddess of childbirth was Lucina, because she brought babies into the light of life.

A modern German word for light is *Licht*, in English Light. We wish to avoid being slavishly literal here, but to speak of language evoking images, we may think as Lisa being both her name, and a word suggesting light.

As a sort of blurry composite, we can visualize (and assume that Leonardo intended this) a title that he may have passed along indirectly to the painter and art historian Giorgio Vasari (1511-1574).

Thematic

During the Renaissance, these were the conventional tropes that the inconographers of West and East were always apt to deliver: Christian religious themes on the one hand, and Classical themes on the other hand. In the Sistine Chapel, for that matter, the ceiling is covered by an attempted conciliation of Tanakh (Jewish Bible) and Classical Mythological themes.

Leonardo obviously was after much larger game. We think that he delivered a finished version to Francesco no later than about 1506. In support of this is the major issue of side-columns. These were something of a convention at the time. Raphael, a famous contemporary, came into possession of some sketches attributed to Leonardo in preparing to paint Lisa Gherardini for her husband. The Giocondo painting appears to have a column on each side of the sitter, whereas scholarship has now proven no such columns exist in the painting that hangs in the Louvre. So what possessed Leonardo to keep redrawing this image for the next fifteen years or so, until his death?

Two Versions: A Second Painting

What we propose, from the research available to us, is that Leonardo's obsession with the portrait of Lisa Gherardini went beyond his delivery of the portrait to her husband sometime around 1503-05. Francesco del Giocondo was celebrating the fruitfulness of his third wife (the earlier two young wives having tragically died giving birth, as was common before modern hygiene and medical understanding).

Lisa, in her mid-twenties, had already borne five children, of whom one died as a baby girl in 1499. Her enigmatic expression and mysterious smile are not difficult to explain. We see both the triumph and gratitude of the survivor, and the melancholy of the mother who not long ago lost her child. We find hints of joy and gratitude around her smile, even playfulness, yet a tinge of melancholy around the eyes.

We can be sure that Leonardo delivered this commission to Francesco del Giocondo as paid and contracted, since there is no record of any legal action against him by del Giocondo.

We agree with scholars who feel the first painting was lost over time, but Leonardo created a second, private version from his notes and sketches from the first Lisa Gherardini portrait.

From about 1503 to his death in 1519, Leonardo obsessed privately over creating a new version of the painting, for his own spiritual purposes.

So if the image remains that of Lisa, then what drove Leonardo to compulsively keep painting, in oil, *sfumato* (smoky) and layered, without pay, and without any commission, for the rest of his life?

ಬ • ಚ

Scientific studies have determined that Leonardo created the portrait of Lisa Gherardini del Gioconda in Florence during the period 1503-1506. There is nothing to indicate that he did not receive his payment, and therefore the assumption must be that he delivered the painting to Francesco and his wife as promised.

Oddly, however, where do we get the painting that hangs in the Louvre, which has been in possession of French monarchs since soon after Leonardo's death in 1519? Evidence suggests that Leonardo continued working on the painting throughout the last years of his life, with some special deep passion that finally Wandrous and Vervain were able to identify.

From sketches done by Raphael and other contemporaries, it is possible to conclude that there was an earlier version of the painting—which Leonardo gave to Francesco and Lisa as promised, on schedule. That other version, whose fate is unknown, apparently was a bit wider, and had columns on either side of the subject (Lisa). Careful examination has shown that the Louvre version brought to France by Leonardo, and completed or nearly completed by around 1516, did not have side columns.

According to Wandrous, the evidence strongly suggests that for some reason, Leonardo kept his sketches and studies of Lisa, and created a new painting of her. Working in oils, he could cover layer after layer as he continued making minute modifications. The painting is especially renowned for introducing a technique called in Italian *sfumato*, meaning smoky.

ಬಂ ● ೞ

We know, from sketches done by Raphael and other contemporaries, that the portrait originally finished for Francesco del Gioconda most likely was flanked by images of classical columns. These would be a convention of the times, both framing the subject, and also signaling wealth, power, culture, and awareness of Classical themes (this being the Renaissance, or re-awakening of lost Classicalism).

It has been proven by scholars in modern times that the Mona Lisa in the Louvre was painted without flanking columns.

From the evidence accumulated over centuries, it appears that Leonardo felt a great passion, lasting until the end of his life, to use his notes and sketches to recreate the painting in a new version, without its original flanking columns.

So the driving question is, why did he work without commission or notoriety, very privately, on this great art work that has become the most expensive and famous painting of all time? What private passion drove him to obsess over the Mona Lisa, which in later centuries would fascinate the entire world.

ಬಂ ● ೞ

The answer is found in Leonardo's heart, beginning with what may be a somewhat unusual gender orientation that is as yet unidentifiable. To simply class him as a sodomist (as in the indictment) is specious. Looking at his overall life—the beauty of both male and female figures he renders in his work; his meticulous scientific studies of everything from cadavers to moonscapes, from tidal dynamics to the fluid properties of light and shadow, and so many grand inquiries; and his relations with his assistants; from those sorts of things, we may conclude that Leonardo was a very loving, tender, yet undefinable man.

His striving was to an idealized divine, which he evidently found (remember, he was a Renaissance man) in ancient Classical mythologies whose study had been in a process of rebirth or rediscovery since 1300. At 1500, with enormous changes taking place in the world—just to mention the voyage of Christopher Columbus to Hispaniola in 1492 as one—Leonardo's world was moving from the Renaissance into an early modern age prefiguring the Industrial Revolution and many social and cultural changes.

Having already painted with brilliance and devotion the Virgin Mary and similar accepted themes approaching or capturing a female divine, it is only a logical step for him to transcend mortality, violence, treachery, all the misery of Renaissance Italy and the world in general, and look to the heavens at the models that the ancients took as their divinities: namely, the sun, the moon, and the stars, taking them in a secular direction to be echoed by the yet-to-come scientific and humanistic Enlightenment that still lay many generations in the future.

As a person, Leonardo remains enigmatic in his own right today. He never married, there is no indication of any major involvement with a woman at any time in his life, and the only brief hint of gendered otherness comes in a fleeting moment when his about 24, and he and several young aristocratic male companions were accused under a vague charge, quickly dismissed, of sodomy. Whether he was naturally gay, straight, bisexual, or otherwise genderous will never be known. It is clear, however, that he was a man of great integrity, deep affections, and of course monumental artistic talent as well as scientific reasoning skills.

Whatever we want to think of Leonardo, or of Lisa, we can take this a step further by deconstructing the painting. We can still detect some of the underlying mechanics in how Leonardo arranged the Mona Lisa, as the following notes will suggest.

Renaissance Classical Themes: Mene (Moon)

We suggest that as he aged, as he came to understand his own mortality, he reached through Renaissance themes (a combination of Christian conventions plus ancient mythologies) to a higher feminine truth.

Representations of Classical imagery reappeared in Renaissance art, not that they had ever really been absent.

Long before the Enlightenment, before the Age of Reason, before Science, it was customary to look to the heavens for understanding and auguries. Before astronomy, astrology was the way in which humans interpreted what they saw in the heavens every day. Since the Old Stone Age, humans had been dazzled by the two most prominent features in the heavens: sun and moon.

As the notes and sketches of Prof. Wandrous and Master's Candidate Claudette Vervain suggest, Leonardo da Vinci, being as fascinated with spiritual and philosophical questions as he was with scientific and technological investigations, sought to capture something of the eternal feminine by using his profound character study of the complex Lisa Gherardini (grateful survivor, proud woman, satisfied wife, universal feminine, yet grieving mother who has lost a child) as a springboard to go one level further. That, as an aside beyond the immediate scope of these notes, echoes themes in other mystical systems, including that of the Jewish Kabbalah.

In Western mythology, the moon has usually been associated with feminine themes. There are of course some exceptions in which these roles are reversed. In modern German, the moon is masculine (*der Mond*) whereas the sun is feminine (*die Sonne*). Many Asian cultures have similar traditions, like Japan's Shinto key sun deity Amaterasu, who is essentially mother of the universe, while the male moon is a lesser god.

Generally, in Western tradition, the sun (e.g., Apollo) is male, and the moon (Artemis, Aphrodite, Venus, Diana, Luna, and many other attributions) is feminine or has feminine attributes. Another Hellenic name is Selene ('bright,' as in Helen, the one of Troy), and a famous variation of Selene is Mene, also a moon goddess.

Notebooks

From his notebooks (as noted also in *Markings*, next) we know that Leonardo believed the moon harbored landscapes much as did the earth he knew, primarily of peninsular Italy. The gardens behind the Mona Lisa could be a typical Renaissance Italian palace garden or manorial hunting forest. However, from our study of the painting, we propose that he has painted his concept of a lunar landscape, self-illumined in a sort of metaphoric mirror image, by the moon herself (*Mond, Luna, Mene, Mona*). While the German word *Mond* is masculine, the feminine tradition in Classical mythology prevails and resonates in this theory.

Markings on the Moon

Though he did not possess the advantage of an optical device (the telescope would not be known until after 1600), Leonardo had a keen eye. Persons of his time did not yet understand that the markings seen on the moon were shadows of craters, mountains, and other topological features. Leonardo did however, in his notebooks, draw confident conclusions that the moon must have air, and water, and therefore life much like that on earth. It is entirely logical to understand the gardens behind Lisa Gherardini (the woman in the painting) as being on the lunar surface. Almost metaphorically, that landscape is mirror-lit or backlit by the face of the moon herself, reflecting the divine solar light (or whatever rationalist interpretation Leonardo might privately attribute to his dangerous and potentially heretical investigations).

Conclusion

That is the great secret of the *Mona Lisa*. Her name is ambiguous. The German word for moon in Mond, and the name Lisa can easily be conflated with the same Indo-European root that gives us the German word *Licht* or the English *Light*, as in Latin *lux*. Taking aside various ambitious and not implausible translations ('mona' or 'monna' as aunt in Italian, and so forth) we may also follow Professor Wandrous' and Claudette Vervain's theory to its conclusion that the title of the painting really means **Radiant Moon**.

20. Appendix 2: Drawings of the Moon

Figure 1: a fair reproduction of the Mona Lisa as seen in the Louvre Museum, Paris (Wandrous Catalogue #101).

Figure 2: Face of Mona Lisa cropped to 4x4 inches (Cat#107). The crosshairs a, a' and b, b' are to establish a fairly exact center of the image in Figure 2 (not marked, but should be z). The line or chord c, c' closely matches what almost looks like a *ferronnière* (headband, minus jewel) of Lisa Gherardini in the portrait. If we did a closer match, we would find that the line of the ferronnière closely matches the visible perimeter of (tangent to) the lunar sphere.

Figure 3: Full moon (NASA) with crater Tycho brightest object lower left of center. Reduced to a matching 4x4 inches. Darkest areas are maria (Cat#207).

Figure 4: superimposed image of *Mona Lisa* on Full Moon at about 33% foreground over 100% background (Cat#208). Notice that the centerpoint of the lips matches the crater Tycho, and her smile radiates outward in all directions, as do the rays of the lunar crater. The maria may serve as rough (impressional) shadings for facial features.

Figure 5: cropped Fig. 5 to draw out emphatic central face area (Cat#209). Same as Fig. 5 but closeup of central facial area. Notice how perfectly Tycho lines up with the philtrum or medial cleft (the furrow running from the center of the upper lip to the cartilaginous septum forming the central divider between the nostrils.

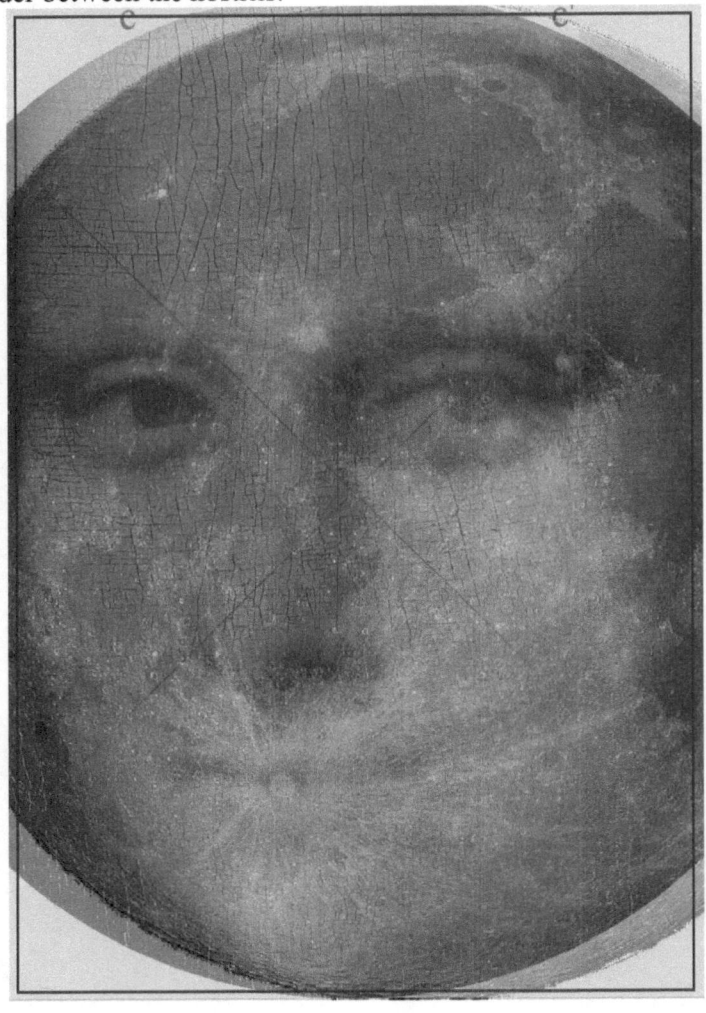

Figure 6: cropped Fig.5 to draw out emphatic central face area (Cat#212). The angle of the portrait is slightly sideways, with Lisa looking to the left of the portrait (her right). See next page for analysis.

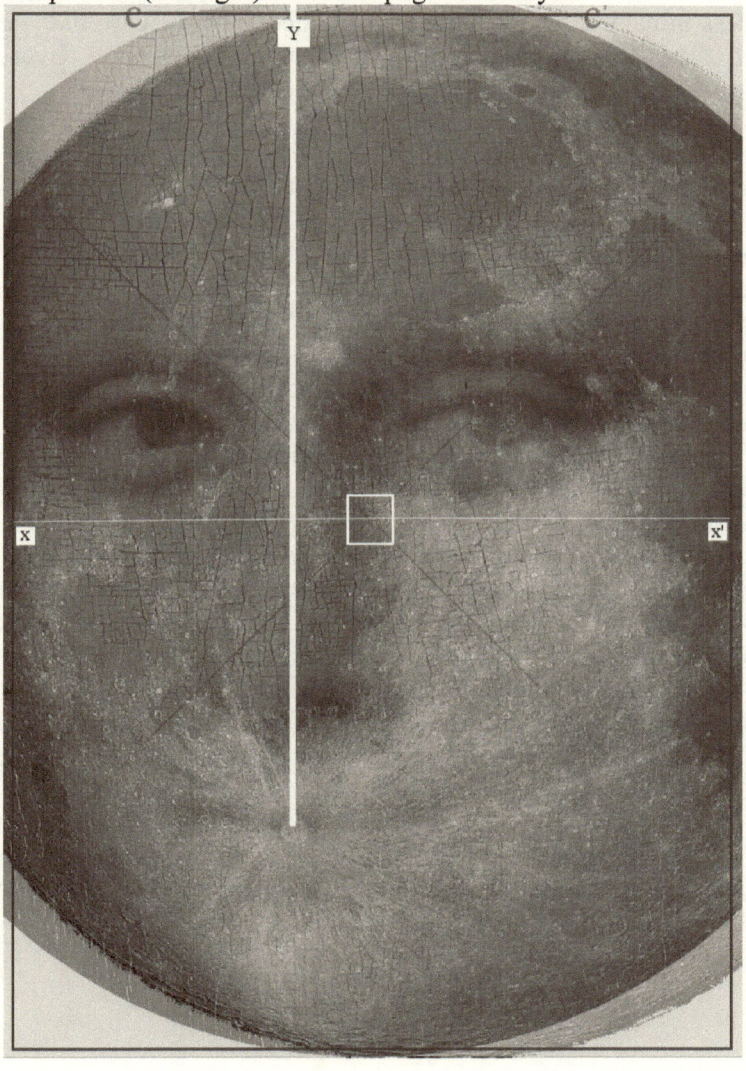

This second painting of Lisa Gherardini was yet another spectacular original work by Leonardo, like his other technological and scientific insights. As a spiritual exercise, he posits a Woman in the Moon, which evokes his own gender ambivalence, but more importantly expresses a recognition of the Goddess in nature, who has been sublimated from a figure like Venus to the sacred *Theotokos* (God-bearer) Holy Mary of Christianity. Ever a fearless truth-seeker, Leonardo again smashes boundaries and dogmata.

These measurements are fairly rigorous (est. 95% tolerance of exactitude), though preliminary. Leonardo worked without modern optical aids (like the telescope, invented a century later).

Regard the line c, c' which is a sort of *ferronnière* matching the upper horizon of the moon at this angle or attitude. This is the angle to which Leonardo first sketched, and then painted, her features to match what he saw on the moon. Mona Lisa (Moon Radiant, Moon Light) becomes his spiritual interpretation of the feminine moon, a kind of Woman in the Moon as opposed to a Man in the Moon as commonly perceived in Western mythologies (a rabbit and other images in non-Western mythologies).

Regard the vertical line y (y, y' implied, with y at top). The Y axis lies 90 degree perpendicular to the ferronnière (c, c') at top. The implied Y' at bottom anchors upon crater Tycho.

Notice the horizontal line X, X' that passes through the central point Z of our original crosshairs A, A' and B, B'. A vertical line at Z (implied, not shown) would be the theoretical center if Lisa were facing straight toward us. Her aspect, however, turns to her right slightly, and we leave it up to more precise measurers to determine the angle of aversion. But notice, most importantly, that the vertical axis Y (with Y' implied at Tycho) passes precisely down her forehead, and down the center of her nose and philtrum, to the crater Tycho at the center of her mouth and lips.

QED: Lisa Gherardini, in Leonardo's obsessed work using her image and the full moon, becomes the Woman in the Moon. This should not be taken trivially, but as a profound spiritual exploration by Leonardo da Vinci. We may then take the painting's name *Mona Lisa* to mean:

Radiant Moon.

For more information and other titles, please visit the website of Clocktower Book at

www.clocktowerbooks.com.

You can also visit our special project for books about Paris, called Books About Paris (originally Paris Bookshop). On the Reserve page, look for at least four novels related to Paris, written by Jean-Thomas Cullen.

www.booksaboutparis.com

www.ingramcontent.com/pod-product-compliance
Lightning Source LLC
Chambersburg PA
CBHW051838170626
46807CB00003B/1238